His eyes blazed int...

She finished drinking her water and didn't bother to comment.

"Okay, how about this. If I kiss you and you feel nothing then I will walk away."

"What?" She knew that wasn't about to happen because she still couldn't forget the kiss he'd given her last night. "London, go home. We can try to come up with a different solution tomorrow." She quickly moved around him and headed toward her bedroom. Feeling self-conscious, she desperately needed to run a comb through her hair. Instead of leaving as she had ordered, London followed her.

"I thought I asked you to leave."

"It's too late for that. We're already engaged."

"Well, I want to be unengaged." There was no way she could be married to him. Not with the way she felt about him. He moved closer. She tried to put some distance between them but his body was positioned in such a way that she was trapped between him and a wall.

"I don't think that's really what you want." He pulled her into his arms and before she could take her next breath, his mouth came down on hers. On contact she released a sigh of surrender. Immediately she softened against him. She closed her eyes and when he touched the tip of his tongue with hers she forgot he was simply trying to prove a point. All she wanted was to taste him.

Books by Angie Daniels

Kimani Romance

The Second Time Around
The Playboy's Proposition
The Player's Proposal
For You I Do

ANGIE DANIELS

is an award-winning author of twelve works of romance and women's fiction. A chronic daydreamer, she knew early on that someday she wanted to create page-turning stories of love and adventure. Born in Chicago, Angie has spent the past twenty years residing in and around Missouri, and considers the state her home. Angie holds a masters in human resource management. For more on this author you can visit her Web site at www.angiedaniels.com.

For you i Do

ANGIE DANIELS

KIMANI™
ROMANCE

This book is dedicated to all of the readers who love the
Beaumont family as much as I do. This one's for you!

KIMANI PRESS™

ISBN-13: 978-0-373-86113-2
ISBN-10:   0-373-86113-3

Recycling programs
for this product may
not exist in your area.

FOR YOU I DO

www.kimanipress.com

Printed in U.S.A.

Dear Reader,

Welcome back to Sheraton Beach, Delaware, where the people are friendly, the men are gorgeous and love is always in the air!

I want to thank all of you for your e-mails, letting me know how much you love those fine Beaumont brothers, Jabarie, Jace and Jaden. Now it's time for their feisty little sister, Bianca.

Bianca is all set to marry a man she thinks is her soul mate when London breaks some life-changing news. Now the irresistible London has every intention of proving to Bianca *he* is the better choice. Get ready for a lot of head-butting, but once these two get together it's going to be hot, hot, hot!

I've grown to love this family and hope you have, too. They'll be back. I promise. Curl up in a chair and get ready for another fabulous trip to the beach.

Enjoy!

Angie Daniels

Chapter 1

"You're doing what?"

Bianca Beaumont's eyes traveled around to all the faces seated at the dining room table. *Maybe this wasn't such a good idea,* she thought as she took in the startled look of her overly dramatic mother and the pissed-off expressions on each of her brothers' faces. The only person who looked like he wasn't opposed to the idea was her father.

Roger Beaumont had fallen asleep.

Jessica Beaumont nudged him in the arm. "Roger, wake up! Did you hear what your daughter just said?"

With a startled snort, Roger sat up straight in the chair and his head snapped in the direction of his wife. "What? What did I miss?"

Jessica rolled her eyes with disapproval, then centered her attention on their only daughter as she spoke, pointing a long accusing finger in Bianca's direction.

"*Your* daughter just announced that she's getting married."

Bianca sighed inwardly. As far as her mother was concerned, she was always her father's child when she was in trouble.

"Married!" Roger barked and then was suddenly wide awake. "I didn't even know you were dating."

"Neither did we," Jace said. "Young lady, you've got a lot of explaining to do."

"Yes, you do," the other two J's replied simultaneously.

Once again, Bianca reluctantly slid her gaze across the table at the grim looks on their faces. Jace, Jabarie, and Jaden. All three of her brothers were overly protective. That was the main reason she'd kept her six-month relationship with Collin a secret.

It didn't matter that she had turned twenty-five two months ago or that she owned a town house, had a great job and paid all her bills. The three J's still tried to dictate how she lived. They were married and she had hoped that once they had families they would stop trying to control her life and focus on making babies with their wives. Speaking of wives…desperately, Bianca looked over at the beautiful women, who usually jumped to her defense, for help. Jace's wife Sheyna looked as if she wasn't sure how to respond to Bianca's announcement, while Danica and Brenna shrugged as if to say, "You're on your own with this one, kid."

"Well?" Jabarie said impatiently. "We're waiting."

Bianca lowered her gaze to the ruby ring on her left hand, hoping for the strength. Tomorrow it would be replaced with a beautiful solitaire. She had been hiding her engagement for almost a week, waiting for the right time to break the news to her family. She'd thought Thursday would be the perfect night. Now she wasn't so sure.

There had been an unspoken rule in their home for as long as she could remember that no matter how busy any of them were, the family always met on Thursdays for dinner at Beaumont Manor. Keeping that in mind, Bianca knew that announcing an engagement was something that needed to be done during a family meeting. She knew that as soon as she stepped out of the room, her family's tongues would wag and by noon tomorrow every person in the small town of Sheraton Beach would know that she was getting married.

"Sweetie, who's the lucky man?"

Bianca looked over at Jabarie's wife, Brenna, and she nibbled her lower lip. "I'm not ready to share that information yet," Bianca said uncertainly.

"Not ready to share?" her father snapped through his teeth. "Why the hell not!"

"Who are his parents?" her mother asked. To Jessica Beaumont, nothing was more important than one's family connections.

"They're dead," Bianca replied and it took everything not to laugh at the appalled look on her mother's face.

"I'm still waiting to find out this young man's name!" her father said impatiently.

Bianca looked over at him with loving eyes. She adored her father. She knew his bark was far worse than his bite. And yet, she had to stand firm in her decision. Giving up Collin's name before it was time to walk down the aisle was the last thing she was going to do.

After dabbing the corners of his mouth with a linen napkin, Jaden asked, "Why is this the first time we've ever heard of him?"

Jaden, the youngest of the three Beaumont brothers, had always been Bianca's favorite. At least that's what she thought before he gave her that long, disapproving look.

"Because none of you have ever approved of any of the men I've dated." And because she didn't want her parents or her brothers—*especially* her brothers—to meet or even know her fiancé's background until after they were married. Otherwise, they would do everything in their power to stop the wedding from ever happening. And there was no way in the world she could allow that to happen. Her future depended on it.

Jabarie gave a short chuckle that lacked humor. "You want to know why we never approve? Because, Bianca dear, you have terrible taste in men."

Pauline, her parents' maid of twenty years, and as far as all the Beaumonts were concerned, a member of the family, returned with a fresh pitcher of cold ice water. Bianca handed over her glass and Pauline refilled it and handed it back to Bianca.

"Thank you," Bianca said then took a sip and another, waiting for the uneasiness in her stomach to settle. Stalling, she sipped from her glass, which kept her from commenting. Okay, so maybe she didn't have the best track record with men and maybe she did have a bad habit of picking up what her brothers labeled as "losers," but they couldn't say any of her boyfriends weren't ever nice to her, or had any *real* issues. Okay, maybe one or two, but that was neither here nor there. This time she was in love. She was certain of it, or at least that's how she would have described what she felt.

Do you really know what love is?

She didn't trust herself to answer. Quickly, Bianca sat up in her chair. Now was not the time to start second-guessing herself. She loved Collin and no matter what her family thought, she was going to marry him.

"Sweetheart, how can I plan a wedding without a name?" her mother asked in a high-pitched whine.

"Easy, Mother. All he has to do is show up," Bianca said with a defensive tilt of her chin. "I'm not about to disclose his identity because I know how all of you think," she said and pointed her finger at every member of the family, sitting around the mahogany table, large enough to comfortably seat thirty people. "The three J's will try to track him down for one of their little talks. And you, Daddy, will hire a private investigator and dig up every single parking ticket that man has ever gotten. Well, I'm not letting that happen this time." She had been through it enough times to know how the four men in her family operated.

"And you, dear mother, all you care about is me finding someone who makes *you* look good. Well, this time I'm doing things my way." On the verge of tears, she reached down for her fork and brought her salad to her mouth.

Jessica gasped. "Bianca, you're my daughter. All I ever wanted was for you to be happy."

Bianca swallowed the lettuce that was suddenly stuck in her throat. "I *am* happy."

Roger raked a frustrated hand across his face the way he always did when he was trying to stay calm. "Honey, please understand why we are all upset. You can't just spring information like this on us," he said, his voice a touch cooler than before. "We don't know his name. Does he even have a job? Sweetheart, come on, tell me something."

Okay, that was reasonable enough. Nodding, she finished chewing then said, "He's a staff sergeant in the air force."

"The military!" her father cried. His eyes widened at the revelation.

Letting her napkin to fall to the table, her mother sat there staring at Bianca. Gaze narrowed, her lips pursing in disapproval. "Please tell me this is some kind of practical joke," she finally said.

Jace shook his head then got up from his seat and made a show of looking under the table.

"A soldier? How's he going to be able to support you?" Jabarie demanded to know.

Bianca sat up, tall and proud. There was no way she was going to allow her family to put down her boyfriend—oops— her fiancé.

She met her brother's hard look. "He's not a soldier," she shot back. "My fiancé's an *airman*. And we'll be fine. In fact, we'll be better than fine. You forget, big brother, I do have a job." As marketing director of the Beaumont Corporation, she received a handsome salary.

"Not to mention a trust fund," Jaden mumbled under his breath.

Bianca's brow rose suspiciously as she gasped. "Are you implying he's only marrying me for my money?"

"Since we haven't met him, we don't know why he's marrying you, now do we?" Jaden challenged.

It was days like today that she hated being the youngest. It wouldn't have mattered if Collin were rich. The three J's would still have found some reason or other to hate him. The idea that he was in the U.S. Air Force was even worse, as far as her parents were concerned. Jaden, the rebellious child, had joined the army right after high school, and her parents had practically had heart attacks. After three years, Jaden decided the military wasn't for him and went on to buy his own body shop. Her parents weren't too crazy about that career choice, either, but after being estranged from their youngest son for years, they had finally learned to accept it. To the four of them, that day was monumental. Because up until that point, as far as their father was concerned, his children had two choices—going to college and working for the Beaumont Corporation, preferably both.

"Do you love him?"

For the briefest moment, Bianca looked over at Danica,

Jaden's wife and a former runway model. She then allowed her gaze to travel around the table. Everyone turned in their seats and all eyes were on her, waiting for her answer.

"Well, young lady?" her father replied impatiently.

Bianca felt her face flush with heat. Dropping her hands to her lap, she rubbed her sweaty palms across her napkin. Then out the corner of her eye, she saw Sheyna wink at her. To her right, Brenna was wearing a look of amusement. Thank God for sisters-in-law. Having them on her side gave her the strength she needed.

Bianca cleared her throat and said, "Of course I love him."

Sheyna clapped her hands with glee. "Then it's settled. We've got a wedding to plan!"

Jace gave her a warning look. Never one to be easily intimidated, Sheyna gave her husband a dismissive wave, then went back to eating her steak.

Roger held up his hands, palms forward. "Wedding? Wait, let's not jump the gun. We need to meet this man first." Her father was clearly not pleased.

"Okay." Bianca said and nodded. What he was asking wasn't unreasonable at all. "He's out of town, but I was planning to bring him to dinner next Thursday. Really I was," she added when she saw the look of disbelief on Jace's face. "I just wanted to let you know first before I walked in the door and said, 'Hey, everybody, meet my fiancé.'"

Her mother gave a rude snort. "Thank you for sparing us the embarrassment."

Pauline came in carrying dessert and the conversation around the table quieted to a low rumble which was fine with Bianca. At least the worst of it was over.

Or almost. She still had something else she needed to tell them, but now was definitely not the time.

Chapter 2

"How did it go?"

Bianca had barely stepped into her town house when she heard the telephone ring. A glance down at the caller ID showed that her best friend, Debra Anderson, was calling.

"About as I expected," she began as she took a seat on the end of her king-size bed and removed her red leather pumps. "Mother faked a heart attack and the three J's acted like they were my daddy."

"Poor Bianca. What did dear old dad have to say about your announcement?"

Bianca rose from the bed with a snort. "You must be talking about when he wasn't asleep."

"You father was asleep?" She could tell that Debra was trying to hold in her laughter.

"Oh, my goodness, yes! Can you believe he was sitting there at the dinner table seconds away from his face falling into the mashed potatoes. If it weren't so serious, I might have laughed."

Unable to contain herself, Debra chuckled lightly into the

receiver. "Sorry, sweetie, but just thinking about it I can't help but to laugh. What did he finally have to say?"

"Not too much because the three J's said it all. Of course, they all wanted to know why this was the first time they had heard about me seeing someone."

Debra paused for a moment then said, "Well, you can't blame them for being curious."

Bianca blew out a frustrated breath as she walked across the plush cranberry carpeting, out of the room and down a long hallway. "I know, but why can't they just be happy for me?"

"Because they're your family and they love you. That's why. All they care about is your happiness."

Scowling, Bianca made her way into the kitchen and removed a bottle of water from the stainless-steel refrigerator, then closed the door and leaned back against the granite countertop. "No, they don't. My brothers don't want to see me with anyone unless they approve of him first."

"Is that what this is really about?"

"Of course not, and you know it."

There was a pregnant pause. "Yes, I know."

Bianca screwed the top off the bottle and took a thirsty swallow before saying, "Let's change the subject. I want to hear how your date went with Brad."

Debra burst into another peal of laughter. "Girl, it was a joke. That man better make sure he loses my number. Do you know he waited until the waiter returned with the bill to tell me that because I had eaten more than he had in his budget for the evening, I needed to help him pay the bill?"

It was Bianca's turn to laugh until she had tears in her eyes. "No, he didn't!"

"Yes, the cheap bastard did, and the bill was barely twenty-five dollars."

"I hate to admit it, Debra, but you do eat too much," she said with amusement.

"I can't help it if I like food," she replied defensively.

"Yeah, but obviously he had been banking on your only ordering a salad."

Debra huffed. "Then that's his problem. Anyone can look at

these hips and know a salad is one thing on the menu I'm not going to order. Now I know why he only ordered a glass of water and a plate of chicken wings."

Bianca chuckled again. She loved living vicariously through her best friend. Her voluptuous friend had curves everywhere it counted and a dynamic personality to match. Men migrated to her and the twenty-six-year-old had a date penciled in for almost every weekend of the month. The problem was that as soon as Debra got home, she was deleting their number from her cell phone or blocking them from calling her house.

Bianca loved Debra, truly she did, but she didn't think Debra was selective enough. She believed that if Debra picked and chose and got to know a little more about a man, other than his first name, she would save herself a lot of time and disappointment.

"I've about given up on men in Delaware," Debra admitted with a discouraging sigh.

"Maybe it's time for you to try Maryland," Bianca suggested, then took another swallow.

"Been there, done that. I think I need to move to the West Coast."

Her comment almost made Bianca choke. "Don't you dare even think about moving away! Then who would I have to complain to?"

"Ha! You know I can't go anywhere. My business is just taking off."

Sinfully Delicious was Debra's catering business. Debra had always been a fabulous cook, and her repeat clientele was definitely proof of that. She had barely been in business a year and already her calendar was booked more than six months in advance.

Bianca pushed away from the counter and moved back down the hall, then headed into her master bathroom and over to a large tub. "You'll be rich before you know it."

"I don't know about that, but at least now I can afford to hire an assistant."

"Oh, Debra! That's great," Bianca said as she turned on the water and poured in a capful of bubbles.

"Yeah, I should be fully staffed in time to cater your wedding reception."

"Ooh, I can't wait to see the look on my mother's face," she said, chuckling.

"Oh, yeah, especially when I prepare a pot of collard greens and ham hocks."

They shared another laugh. If those dishes were on Bianca's wedding reception menu, Jessica Beaumont would definitely have a heart attack for real.

"I'd better let you go. When are you taking lover boy to meet the family?"

"I told them at dinner that I was bringing him next week. But I lied. I'm waiting until the week before our wedding. He can meet all of them at once. You want to come?"

"I wouldn't miss it for the world. We'll see if he passes the test. You know we have to assess."

"Everything will be fine," Bianca said with a chuckle. "I'll talk to you tomorrow."

Bianca disconnected and put down the phone. Still wearing a smile, she slipped out of her dress and returned to her private bathroom, decorated beautifully with mauve and cream tile. She was dying to enjoy a hot, soothing bath and then get into her pajamas and curl up under the cool sateen sheets. Dinner with her family was usually full of surprises, but today was the first time in a long time that she had been the focus of attention.

I'm getting married.

It was still hard for her to believe that at twenty-five she was tying the knot, as the last of the Beaumont children to marry. Within a four-year period, even her die-hard bachelor brothers, Jace, Jabarie and Jaden, had all fallen in love and gotten married.

She climbed into the tub and leaned back on her inflated pillow, then closed her eyes and laid there for the longest time, just thinking about her reasons for keeping her marriage to Collin a secret.

They had met in a small coffee shop on the beach. The attraction had taken time but eventually she and Collin had spent almost every waking moment together. Collin made her laugh. He was affectionate, considerate and great in bed. Most important, she loved him. Taking a deep breath, she sank lower in the tub and began imagining her life with Collin. The honeymoon.

Buying a house together. Planning a life. After a while Bianca stopped feeling guilty. Considering the circumstances, her family was just going to have to find a way to get over it.

A half hour later, wrapped in a towel, she padded on bare feet back into her bedroom, picked up her phone and hit speed dial.

"Hey, sweetheart."

Bianca took a seat on her thick cream comforter and smiled at the sound of Collin's low husky voice. "Hey, yourself."

"How did things go with your family?"

"About the way I expected. They flipped."

Collin breathed heavily in the phone. "I should have been there with you."

"I know, but you understand why I needed to do this alone."

"Yes, but I need to meet them, Bianca."

"Yes, and you will. I already told them I would be bringing you to dinner."

He gave a sigh of relief. "Good. I can't wait to meet them."

"And they can't wait to meet you," she said. She could already see her mother sizing him up from across the table.

"How about I drive over tomorrow and we have dinner?" he suggested.

"That sounds good to me."

"Get some rest. I love you."

Her lips curled upward. Everything was going to be okay. She could feel it. "I love you, too," she finally said.

Bianca returned the phone to the cradle then got ready for bed. "Everything is going to be all right," she said. Falling back on the bed, Bianca wished she felt as confident as she sounded.

"Jaden, sweetheart, please come to bed."

"I will in a minute," he replied and continued to pace back and forth the length of their bedroom.

Danica laid down the romance novel she had been reading and watched her husband wear out her Berber carpet. "I'll admit that your sister's announcement caught us all by surprise, but Bianca *is* a grown woman."

"I'm not saying she isn't, but *engaged?* Come on, Danica. We haven't even met this dude."

She shrugged and smiled lovingly at her husband. "Love happens like that some times."

Jaden stopped abruptly and looked over at her lying across the bed. "I'm not buying it."

The room rang with her soft laughter. "You don't have a choice. Your sister is set on getting married whether the three of you like it or not. Besides, unless you've forgotten, we fell in love in less than a month."

"That's different."

"What's different about it?" she challenged and met Jaden's intense stare. After several long seconds he scowled, then started pacing again.

"What do we know about this guy? We don't even know who he is or where he comes from. He's probably after her money."

"Then again, maybe he truly loves her."

"You're not helping."

She gave him a scolding look. "No, I'm not. Because you're not being reasonable. Your sister is old enough to make her own decisions."

Jaden shook his head. "You don't know my sister the way I do. She has a habit of making bad choices, particularly when it comes to men."

"But she's a grown woman, and we all make mistakes until we finally find that perfect man."

Danica rose from the bed and Jaden froze in his tracks when her robe fell in a pool around her feet. His eyes traveled up the length of her mile-long legs and he took a deep breath as his eyes took in the pale pink negligee with a slit in the front, displaying her swollen belly. As far as Jaden was concerned, at six months' pregnant, Danica was sexier than ever. Slowly, she sashayed over to her husband and pressed her hand to his bare chest. Jaden immediately wrapped his arms around her waist.

Standing on her tiptoes, she kissed Jaden's lips then leaned back and put her hand on his cheek. "Quit worrying so much. At least give the guy a chance." She raised her mouth to his again and gave him a searing kiss.

Jaden pushed thoughts of Bianca and her fiancé to the back of his mind. He would deal with that issue tomorrow. In the meantime, he scooped Danica into his arms and carried her back to bed. The only thing he was concerned about was properly making love to his wife.

Chapter 3

London looked over the renovation plans for the new restaurant and smiled. It was finally coming true. Clarence's Infamous Chicken and Fish House was finally expanding.

He scowled, then scolded himself for being so excited, because if his father hadn't gotten sick none of this would be happening.

Rising from his chair, he walked into the kitchen and took a beer from the refrigerator, then stepped out onto the deck and stared out over the Atlantic Ocean.

Two years ago his father had suffered a stroke. London had been days away from reenlistment as a technical sergeant in the U.S. Air Force, but after six years decided it was time to come home. After weeks of prayer by London and his sisters, his father, who made a full recovery, decided it was time to enjoy the rest of his life and gladly handed over the family business to his only son. The first things London did were renovate the restaurant, expand the menu to include more down-home cooking and start catering events. In the last year, business had been so good that he and his father decided it was time to open a second restaurant. They found a prime piece of property in New Castle. The former Chinese restaurant had been out of business for almost three years, yet almost all the equipment inside was salvageable. After adding a few improvements to the building and the decor, he would be opening for business in less than two months. *My dream is finally coming true,* he thought with a proud smile. He had dreamed about expanding the business since grade school.

Life definitely couldn't get any better, or could it?

London took a moment to think about that question as he stared out at the night and brought the bottle to his lips. Last week he had had a long phone conversation with his father. As usual, Clarence B. Brown wanted to know when he would settle down and start a family.

London took another sip as his thoughts raced. If he had his way, he would die a bachelor. He took women out, had a good time and rarely gave them a second thought. While he took another swallow, he had to admit that that wasn't entirely true. There was one woman he had known for years who still made his pulse race.

Bianca Beaumont.

The petite beauty was breathtaking. Ever since he'd returned to Sheraton Beach and laid eyes on her as a grown-up, he couldn't stop thinking about her. He remembered her standing beside her brother as he chatted with Jaden. Her short trendy haircut had been perfect for her small oval-shaped face. And when her eyes had fixed on him, the dark walnut coloring was so compelling he couldn't help wondering what color they were when they glowed with passion. And then there was the fullness of her lips and the way they begged to be kissed. Countless nights he found himself thinking about the taste of her on his tongue and fantasizing about burying himself deep inside her welcoming warmth. Unfortunately, Bianca was his best friend's sister, and bedding her was against the rules. Besides, considering the way her brothers acted when a man even looked in her direction, it just wasn't worth the drama. Nevertheless, that didn't stop him from looking.

They had grown up in the same town and even though they didn't move in the same social circles, he hung out with her brother Jaden. Together they graduated high school and enlisted in the military.

Since his return to Sheraton Beach two years ago, he'd run into Bianca off and on, but last year he had the pleasure of dancing with her at Jaden's wedding. He definitely had not expected the rush of pleasure that hit him square in the middle when he had taken Bianca's hand and led her out onto the dance floor. Just moments with her in his arms and London knew that was where she belonged forever. After that night, they had gone out on a couple of occasions, but their evenings had always ended with nothing more than brotherly kisses.

He sighed and wondered why he was even thinking about Bianca. Maybe because he hadn't had a date in weeks. While sipping his beer, London tried to remember the last time he had been intimate with a woman, and after several moments decided it had been way too long. Managing the restaurant and trying to open a second one had kept him too busy for a personal life. At the age of thirty, he loved sex just as much as most men his age did, and would love to someday have a serious relationship with the right woman. But now the timing was wrong. Besides, finding a woman to take him seriously might not be easy. Unfortunately, he had developed a reputation as something of a playboy.

London scowled at the thought. He had never been one to play with a woman's emotions. He made it a habit of letting anyone he became involved with know upfront where she stood with him. Yet few were taken on more than two dates.

Hearing the doorbell, London took a final swig then pushed off from the deck, dropped the bottle in the trash and strolled through the house. He swung the door open just as Jaden was about to ring the doorbell a second time.

"What took you so long?" he barked.

"Hello to you, too," London said as Jaden stepped into his house without waiting for an invitation. "What brings you over?"

Without answering, Jaden moved into the kitchen, looked inside the refrigerator and retrieved a beer. London followed.

"Do I have to have a reason to drop by to see my boy?"

"On a Friday night at nine o'clock when you have a beautiful pregnant wife at home? Of course not." London paused and leaned against the doorway. "I was just getting ready to change clothes and go check out this new club on Birch Drive. You want to hang?"

Jaden paused, screwed off the top on the bottle then shook his head. "Nah."

Laughing, London gave him a knowing smile. "I didn't think so."

Moving away from the refrigerator, Jaden walked over to the table and took a seat opposite his best friend. "Bianca's getting married," he announced without preamble.

London pushed away from the wall and barked, "What?" louder than he'd intended. He felt as if he'd been sucker punched.

"Yep," Jaden said after giving London a weird look. He then shrugged and took a long, thirsty swallow. "She announced it at dinner yesterday."

He struggled to keep his voice steady. "Who's the lucky man?"

Jaden shrugged again as he brought the bottle back to his lips. "Some cat we have yet to meet," he said, frowning.

London rubbed a hand across his head as he gave a strangled laugh. Again he tried to regain his composure. "She's marrying a total stranger?" he asked and stepped farther into the room.

"It seems that way. She refuses to give us any information about him—except that he's in the Air Force."

London nodded and almost sympathized with her decision. He knew Jabarie, Jace and Jaden well enough to understand Bianca's need for secrecy. If Jaden had even thought for a moment anything more had been going on between him and Bianca other than friendship—not that there was—he would have acted like a plumb fool. Unfortunately for him, other than a few goodnight kisses, nothing more had happened.

While Jaden finished his beer, London moved over and straddled the chair across from him and listened while Jaden told him everything about Bianca's announcement at dinner the night before. "Well, I guess congratulations are in order." He didn't know what else to say.

Jaden gave him a cutting look. "Over my dead body. I plan to find out whatever I can about the dude and put a stop to this madness." The venom in his voice matched the expression on his face.

London was pleased to know that he wasn't the only one unhappy about Bianca getting married. "You think he's after her money?" he asked after a long, intense pause.

"Maybe. She says it's love, but I don't buy it," Jaden grumbled, then tilted the bottle again.

It bothered London to even think of Bianca being in love with another man. It was selfish of him, especially since he had no intention of marrying. He just didn't like knowing that she was happy with someone else.

London tamped down the sizzle of jealousy. Bianca was nothing more than a friend to him. "You said he's in the military?" he asked, then watched as Jaden took another sip of beer before putting the bottle down.

He nodded. "That's what she said."

"That should make it easier."

Jaden gave him a sidelong glance. "You think you can find out who he is?"

Jaden knew London was a former security forces investigator. He had ways of finding out things if he needed to know.

"I'll watch her house for her fiancé or his vehicle, then talk to one of my guys at Dover Air Force Base and see what I can find out about him."

"Yo, I'd appreciate whatever information you can find."

London arched his brow. "I'm going to do better than that. If that cat ever got a speeding ticket, I'll know about it before the week is over."

Chapter 4

"You sure you like it?"

Bianca looked up at her fiancé and smiled, warmed by the uncertainty that registered in Collin's liquid-brown eyes. He was always trying to go out of his way to please her. It was one of the qualities she loved most about him. Although, recently it was starting to get on her nerves.

"It's beautiful, really," she said reassuringly, then looked down at the two-carat solitaire surrounded by baguettes. The ring wouldn't have been her first choice, and she would have preferred if he had taken her along to pick it out, but she wasn't complaining. Gazing down her finger once more, she sucked in a deep, shaky breath.

She was now officially engaged to Collin Clark.

"I'm glad." He leaned across the seat of his car and pressed his lips to hers. Bianca closed her eyes and, as the kiss deepened, she waited for the fireworks, the wild flutter in her chest.

Nothing. Absolutely positively nothing.

When the kiss finally ended, Bianca leaned back against the seat and released a heavy sigh.

"Is everything okay?" Collin asked and stared at her with those big, round eyes that she loved so much.

"Yes," she lied and pasted on a smile.

"You sure?" he asked with annoying uncertainty. "I'm not pushing you to marry too soon, am I?"

Under normal circumstances, yes, but not in her case. The sooner they married the better off she would be.

"No, four weeks from now is perfect." Now all she had to do was find a way to keep her family from snooping around in her personal life for that long.

Collin laced her fingers with his. "I don't mean to rush you, but I love you so much and can't wait to make you my wife. I'm just afraid my unit is deploying and I don't want to leave for a year without knowing I have you in my life."

"Sweetheart, really, it's okay." He'd been trying to justify his reasons for rushing their marriage for the last week and it was starting to drive her nuts.

"That's what I love about you most. Your understanding that I have a military obligation." He gave her another kiss, then climbed out of the car, and came around to her side and opened the door. Taking her hand, he helped her out of the car then led her up the walkway toward her door. Bianca noticed that she had forgotten to turn on the light. The porch was dark.

She looked over at him. "You want to go to New York for the weekend? We can check out a Broadway play."

Collin dropped his eyes to the ground then cleared his throat. "I was going to talk to you about that. My unit is sending me to Virginia next Friday to do some training."

Her brow rose. *Why was this the first time he was mentioning this,* she wondered. She looked over at him. The moonlight was obscured by clouds, so she was unable to read the expression on his face to tell if he was as upset as she was. "How long are you going to be gone?"

"Three days," he answered crisply, taking the keys from her hand and leaning around her to unlock the front door. "I should be home by Monday."

Her eyebrows knitted with disapproval. It seemed as if every month his unit was sending him somewhere else.

Sensing her irritation, Collin pulled her into the circle of his arms and dropped a kiss on her forehead. "Don't be mad at me. I know this is last minute, but that's the way it is in the military." He paused and released a frustrated breath. "That's one of the reasons I'm getting out as soon as my enlistment contract is up."

Bianca was relieved to hear that. Since they had begun dating, Collin's unit had him flying all over the country on numerous assignments.

Releasing her, Collin turned the knob and opened the door. Light spilled out from the foyer. "We'll spend some quality time together when I get back."

"I'm not liking this one bit. How about I go with you?" Bianca asked.

Collin gave her an innocent smile. "Baby, you know you can't go with me. I'm an airman. I took an oath to serve my country and that's just the way it is. These are solo missions."

"It doesn't mean I have to like it," she said, pouting.

He pulled her tighter in his arms, pressed his lips to her forehead then pulled back and gazed lovingly down into her eyes. "I know, baby, and we're going to do something special when I get back."

She sighed. He seemed sincerely upset about leaving again and her anger was swallowed by a wave of guilt. It wasn't his fault that his job sent him away so much. Being an airman in the U.S. Air Force was not just what he did, it was who her fiancé was. And instead of being selfish she should be proud of the role he played in serving his country.

"I'm sorry. I'm just getting a little tired of rarely being able to spend a weekend with my fiancé."

He nodded then leaned forward. "We'll do something special when I get back. I promise."

Bianca smiled. She was being ridiculous. "Okay."

He leaned down to brush a kiss over her lips. "Good night."

"How about a limo ride to the airport on Friday? I'll pick you up at your apartment," she asked softly to his retreating back.

When he looked over his shoulder, a smile curled his lips. "That would be great. I'll see you tomorrow."

She walked into the house, showered and put on something

comfortable then moved to the refrigerator. A bottle of white wine was sitting on the top shelf. Frowning, she hesitated, then reached for a bottle of water and headed into the family room. Bianca flopped down on the couch and sat there as her eyes traveled around the room that had become her comfort zone. The walls were a soft peach, the windows were covered with cream-colored vertical fabric blinds with sheer white skirts and the overstuffed couch and love seat were upholstered with peach and cream fabric. The 2,200 square-foot home was her sanctuary. Last year when she decided to move out, her parents tried to come up with every reason why she needed to continue to live with them, but for once Bianca stood her ground and a month later she spotted the town house in a gated community on the outskirts of Sheraton Beach and knew the corner lot with a magnificent view of the ocean had been waiting just for her.

That had been her first claim of independence from her parents.

Growing up under the control of three older brothers, while trying to assert her independence, had been difficult. But for the last year she had not wavered. Though she knew her family loved her and wanted what was best for her, Bianca was ready to finally live her life. That included making decisions about which man she wanted to marry.

Bianca reached for the remote and after turning on the television, she flipped through the channels until she found one of her favorite movies, *Pretty Woman* with Julia Roberts. She sank low into the cushions with a large throw draped across her feet and lost herself in the love story.

Midway through the movie, she released a heavy sigh. For years she dreamed of falling in love the same way as the characters in the movie. But then she realized that *Pretty Woman* was strictly fiction. Love was nothing like that. Or anything like the love stories she read in romance novels.

She loved, respected and admired Collin and his chosen career. But nothing she felt was anything at all like the stories she read. Those stories were all just fairy tales—make-believe.

Glancing over at the five-by-seven photo of her fiancé on the oak end table, she pursed her lips. She was deeply fond of Collin and they would have a good life together. That was what was important. Bianca was certain she would make a wonderful military wife.

As she watched Richard Gere kiss Julia Roberts, she wished it were her. If only Collin made her heart flutter, then she'd be the happiest woman in the world.

But it was too late. Regardless of what doubts she had, she couldn't change her mind now. She had made a promise to him. And then there was that other reason…

Chapter 5

The elevator doors opened on the main floor and Bianca moved across the sparkling-white, marbled lobby of the Beaumont Hotel, leaving behind the sweet, sensual scent of her perfume.

As she passed by, the aroma wafted under London's nose, instantly conjuring up wicked thoughts. Briefly, he lowered his eyelids and inhaled. The scent was as captivating as the woman who wore it.

Tossing aside the newspaper he had been using to shield his face, he settled back into the plush chair he'd occupied in the lobby for the last half hour. With great interest, London watched as Bianca walked over to the front desk to talk to the reception staff.

The manager rushed out of the office behind the desk and was standing there in a black suit, smiling down at his boss with admiration and respect. From where he was sitting, London could hear the manager complimenting Bianca on how fabulous she looked in a paisley suit with black stiletto heels.

An amused smile crossed London's lips. Bianca, and everyone in her family, was treated like royalty in their small town. The Beaumont Hotel was responsible for providing em-

ployment for over twenty-five percent of the residents of
Sheraton Beach and also allowed several local merchants to set
up boutiques in the lobby for a fraction of what it would have
cost anywhere else. Because of that, some residents of Sheraton
Beach were intimidated by them, while others who knew how
much they bolstered the local economy jumped when any of the
Beaumonts snapped their fingers.

Well, most people. The Beaumont Corporation—and all the
money, prestige and privilege associated with it—was definitely
impressive. But it had never intimidated London. After his mother
died, of brain cancer when he was ten, his father had raised him
and his four sisters. The restaurant never made enough to put them
in high society or given them the privileges the Beaumont children
had, but that didn't stop him and Jaden from becoming best friends.

London remembered the first time he had been invited to
Beaumont Manor; he had whistled under his breath at the size of
the house, which was well over nine thousand square feet. He'd
been amazed at the Olympic-size pool in the back. They had private
tennis and basketball courts. It took a month of visits before he
finally got used to the Beaumonts' wealth and realized that they
were just regular folks who happened to have big-time money.

Pushing his memories aside, London focused on Bianca, who
was talking on her cell phone. Since Jaden had dropped by his
house last Friday, London had been following her all over town
and enjoying every minute of it.

While she sat down in a chair in the corner and chatted,
London allowed his mind to travel back nine years to the first
time he'd ever laid eyes on Bianca. She had been sitting at the
kitchen table at Beaumont Manor, holding a pen in the manner
of a cigarette. Sixteen-year-old Bianca had appeared to be deep
in thought, not realizing that she was a being watched.

Even then he knew that Bianca might be that one woman who
might make him think twice about settling down, which was why
it was probably for the best when she stopped answering his
phone calls. He'd wanted a sexual relationship and Bianca had
wanted so much more from a man. Watching her, he wondered
if maybe agreeing to do this favor for Jaden had been a mistake.

Bianca sat with her legs crossed and he admired their shapeliness. The short paisley suit of gold and brown complemented her toasted-pecan complexion. Never one for a lot of jewelry, he was surprised that she was wearing a diamond necklace and matching dangling earrings. A gold watch accented the ensemble. Her short brown hair was combed back away from her face and her makeup was flawless. The red color on her lips was daring him to come across the lobby and kiss her. It was a tempting offer.

London frowned. *He was on a mission,* he reminded himself. He watched as Bianca rose, returned her phone to her purse and waved goodbye to the girl behind the front desk. London stood as she headed to the revolving doors at the entrance of the hotel. Just before she left the elegant hotel, she stopped long enough to look over her shoulder, almost as if she knew she was being watched. London held his breath until Bianca finally turned and moved through the door. After waiting until the count of five, he followed.

London reached the revolving door as the valet helped Bianca into the sleek black limousine. From the other side of the glass, London watched as she climbed gracefully into the car and slid across the smooth leather seat. Bianca crossed her long legs, closed her eyes and inhaled deeply. The valet shut the door and the driver pulled out.

London headed over to his SUV, which he had left in the visitors' parking lot in front of the hotel. He pulled out his keys, climbed in behind the wheel and within seconds was following at a close distance behind the limo. The Beaumont Hotel was located on a hill at the center of town. He followed the vehicle down the slope to the heart of downtown.

While obeying the twenty-mile-an-hour speed limit, his eyes traveled up and down the wide cobblestone streets that were lined with single-story buildings and mom-and-pop stores. Sheraton Beach, a beachfront town with a population of less than five thousand, was ready to come alive in a little over a month when the Memorial Day weekend marked the beginning of the tourist season. Then restaurants would be filled and parking would be next to impossible. Beaches would be packed with tourists eager for a respite from the workday world and a nice tan.

When the airport limo came to a halt on Main Street, London

pulled into an empty parking spot a few yards away and waited. In a matter of seconds, a tall, dark brown man with a beefy frame and a low-fade haircut came into view. He was wearing an air force battle-dress uniform.

Collin Clark.

After spotting his car parked in Bianca's driveway two nights ago, London had run his license plate and discovered her fiancé's name, address and military history. Collin Clark was a twenty-nine-year-old decorated airman who was up for promotion next month. So far he seemed legitimate, but London was still awaiting further information that he should have by the end of the day.

London's fingers tightened around the steering wheel when Bianca climbed out of the vehicle, and threw herself into the man's waiting arms. He watched the two of them share a passionate kiss. He didn't know why it bothered him so much seeing someone else holding her that way, but it did.

The driver came around, took Collin's duffel bag and loaded it in the limousine's trunk, while Collin took Bianca's hand and helped her back into the vehicle. Within minutes they were on their way again.

What was wrong with him? During the next several miles, London's mind was racing with images, wishing it was him in the backseat of the limousine with Bianca. He could only imagine what the two of them were doing as they drove slowly through town and onto a service road, heading in the direction of the airport. It appeared that Collin was going on a little trip, which meant London wouldn't be able to track his whereabouts for the next couple of days.

He followed the couple to the airport and watched Bianca drop him off. Collin climbed out, kissed her goodbye and watched her pull off before heading inside the airport.

As soon as the limousine was around the corner, London pulled into a drop-off spot and put his flashers on. Climbing out of his car, he was ready to risk getting towed to find out where Collin was flying to when he spotted him coming back outside the airport. After looking both ways, a smile curled his lips as he hailed a cab.

With his eyes glued to Collin, London climbed back inside

his SUV and waited until the cab pulled away from the curb, then followed at a safe distance.

When the cat's away, the mice will play. And that's what London was hoping for.

It was showtime.

Chapter 6

It only took a couple of hours for London to discover that Collin was scum.

After leaving the airport, London followed Collin back to his rented apartment. Within minutes after returning, Collin hopped into his parked car and drove away. London followed him to Chester, Pennsylvania where Collin pulled into the driveway of a small ranch home in a new subdivision, where he was greeted at the door by a curvaceous, chocolate beauty. She wrapped her arms around him with a kiss that left very little doubt in his mind that this woman was not Collin's sister.

An hour later, London realized that the two didn't know what closing the blinds meant, because they'd left theirs wide open, making taking photographs easy. He followed Collin all weekend, which was easy because the loser spent the entire time in Pennsylvania with the lovely woman. At the mall. At the movies holding hands, and visiting friends. Sunday afternoon, London finally received a call from a buddy from his old security forces unit, who was now assigned to Dover Air Force Base, and found out that the house was not only Collin's permanent address, but the woman was his wife.

Now he had to find a way to tell Bianca.

That Sunday evening, London was parked in front of her house when his phone rang. Without looking at the ID, he flipped it open.

"London speaking."

"Did you find out anything?"

He closed his eyes at the sound of Jaden's voice, wishing he had checked the caller ID first. "Nothing concrete."

"What does that mean?" Jaden asked impatiently.

He lifted his eyelids in time to watch a light come on in the living room. "It means that I have my suspicions but I need to confirm what I suspect before I tell you what I discovered."

There was a pause. Jaden was not used to being blown off. "I can hear it in your voice. You know something." When London didn't answer, he asked, "He's using my sister, isn't he?"

"Not if I can help it." And London was a man of his word.

On Monday, Bianca came home after a long day at work. She changed into workout shorts and a T-shirt, put on her favorite pair of flip-flops and went into the kitchen for a cup of tea. While the water warmed, she reached in the cookie jar for a couple of shortbread cookies, took a seat and nibbled. Glancing over at the clock on the wall, she noted that she had two hours before she was supposed to leave for the airport to pick up Collin.

Only seconds after the microwave's timer informed her that her water was ready, she heard a car in the driveway. Rising from the chair, she hurried over to the window and peered out between the blinds. A swooshing rush of breath escaped from her parted lips just as her eyes widened in surprise.

London Brown!

What in the world did he want? Not waiting to find out, Bianca quickly hurried out of the kitchen and down the hall to her bedroom. Glancing at her reflection in the mirror, she frowned. Just as she thought, her hair was a mess. Reaching across her dresser, she grabbed a comb and while looking in her vanity mirror, she ran it through her short brown curls and frowned at the way her hair refused to cooperate. Unfortunately, there wasn't anything she could do about it now.

The doorbell rang and Bianca took one final look. If she had known London was coming over, she would have chosen something other than the faded pink T-shirt and spandex shorts. With a sigh, she put the comb down, then headed toward the door as she heard the doorbell again.

"I'm coming. I'm coming," she mumbled under her breath as she moved to the door, the entire time wondering why London was paying her a visit.

"Who is it?" she asked as if she didn't already know.

"It's London." The deep voice sent a spark of excitement straight to her heart. Get a grip. She warned. She didn't know why she behaved that way every time she was around him. *It's not as if I'm attracted to him,* she told herself.

She took a moment to get herself together, then opened the door. "Hello."

"Hey, sexy."

Sexy? Yep, that's exactly how she would have described London Brown. Her eyes swept over him, finding the view to be nothing short of fine. London was standing on her porch and his six-foot frame was silhouetted by moonlight. This particular April evening, he looked hotter than ever. A crisp, black, long-sleeved shirt showcased his solid chest, and together with his black jeans made him look mysterious and daring. Downright sexy, in fact. His thick, close-cropped, wavy black hair added to his devilishly handsome looks. He usually wore a neatly trimmed goatee, but now he had the start of a beard. She figured he was probably too busy juggling dates to spare twenty minutes to go to the barbershop. The stubble on his jaw was smooth and dark, giving him a rakish look that was just too damn appealing.

"Like what you see?"

She felt her cheeks flame. London thought every woman in Sheraton Beach wanted him. *Conceited* was his middle name. There was no denying that he was fine as they came in a polished, Will Smith kind a way, but she preferred a more rugged look, which was why she was attracted to Collin. Nothing was more handsome than a man in a military uniform, she reminded herself.

"Actually, I was thinking you looked a bit scrubby this evening. What, some woman broke your heart and you came running to cry on my shoulder?"

He shot her a disarming smile. "Very funny. My love life has nothing to do with my reason for dropping by to see you."

She crooked an eyebrow at him. London had been to her house before, but not in the last few months. Not since she realized she could no longer control her feelings around him. "What brings you here?"

"Why don't you let me in and I'll tell you," he said, staring down at her with those sexy brown eyes of his that held glints of gold. Every time he stared at her, she felt as if she were in a trance.

It took everything she had to look away. Then she stepped aside and let him in. He brushed past, and the scent of his cologne was enough to make another woman weak at the knees. She was grateful that his back was turned.

Bianca shut the door while London moved across her oak floor into her plush, stylish living room with familiarity. With his hands behind his back, he stared out a bank of floor-to-ceiling windows that showcased an incredible view of a sandy beach and the ocean beyond. And while he stared out the window, Bianca took in the view inside.

She admired his slanting cheekbones and strong nose and his full lips that were made to kiss. He was something that a woman wrote about in her journal, and that was the reason he was all wrong for her. London Brown had a reputation as a heartbreaker, which meant he was off-limits.

When London had returned to town, they had gone out on a couple of occasions. But they hadn't spoken since their last dinner date. London was sexy and knew it. And as soon as word got around that he was back in town, every single woman in Sheraton Beach would be at Clarence's Infamous Chicken & Fish House buying lunch, then returning again for dinner. Hell, if London served breakfast, they would have been there. Bianca thought it was a shame the way those women threw themselves at him. What was even worse was the way London sucked it up through a thin straw. Within weeks, London Brown became a hot commodity and everywhere Bianca turned she saw him with one female after another on his arm or in his car. She just turned up her nose and looked the other way. After a while, she started ignoring his calls and rejecting his gifts. A player was not her style. Ending their relationship had been hard. Unfortunately, London had wanted something she didn't—a no-strings-attached sexual relationship. At the time, Bianca knew there was no way she could have separated her body from her heart.

"I heard about your engagement," London said, then swung around and gave her a bold, daring look.

The sound of his voice jolted Bianca and she gasped, caught completely off guard that he had mentioned it. For some reason it bothered her that he thought she was no longer available. "Who told you?"

He shrugged, then gave her a slow, sexy smile that said the answer was obvious. "Your brother told me."

She held her breath before letting it out slowly. "Which brother? Jaden?" she asked as she walked over to an oversize sofa and lounged comfortably across it. She knew it couldn't have been Jace because he was in Virginia interviewing staff for their new hotel. She had thought about moving to Virginia on several occasions to get away from her demanding mother and her overly possessive brothers, but she never did and now...now that she was getting married there was no point in going anywhere. Especially since Collin was stationed in Delaware.

"It must have been Jaden. He's always running his mouth."

"I'd rather not say." London replied with a chuckle as he strolled around her room past the bookcases on the opposite wall, pausing long enough to browse a title or two from her extensive collection. Bianca gave his back a long, suspicious look. She'd known him long enough to know that this wasn't just a social visit. London had come to her town house for a reason.

She blew out an impatient breath. "I'm really not in the mood for games. What do you want?"

Light brown eyes, a striking contrast to his dark skin, narrowed slightly under raven eyebrows before London reached into the inside pocket of his windbreaker. He removed a manila envelope and tossed it onto a dark oak coffee table. Bianca glanced down at the envelope then up at him again.

"What's that?"

His eyes darkened with an indefinable emotion. "Something I think you need to see."

She hesitated a few seconds longer, as if she feared it was some kind of booby trap, before she finally reached out for the envelope and opened it. For the longest time she stared down at its contents.

Bianca froze as a multitude of emotions ran through her— shock, denial and finally enough anger to cause her body to shake. "Where did you get these?" her voice was barely audible.

"I took them myself."

London captured her gaze and was holding it with an intensity that she found unnerving. He wasn't kidding. Looking down once more in disbelief at photograph after photograph of her fiancé in the arms of another woman, her hands began to shake. Driving in his car. Holding hands. Eating dinner at *her* favorite restaurant in Philadelphia, she felt as if the wind had been knocked out of her. "These aren't real. This must be some kind of joke." But even as she said that, she knew it was not a joke. London would never lie to her. He'd always told it like it was, and she liked how straightforward he was, even when she didn't want to hear the truth. Unlike a lot of men she knew, London had never been afraid to speak his mind. She expected nothing less now. Anger coursed through her. For a second, she'd thought he had dropped by to wish her luck on her future, but instead he'd come to destroy her happiness. Her life.

She sprang from the couch and glared up at the tall man looming over her. "Who asked you to bring these here?"

Lowering his gaze, he said, "No one."

Irritated, she narrowed her eyes at him and fisted her hands at her waist. "You're lying." Her mind was reeling. This couldn't be happening to her. There had to be some kind of misunderstanding. Bile rose from her stomach and threatened to choke her. With grim determination, she forced it back. "Where did you get these?"

"I already told you. I took them."

"Quit saying that. I want to know who took these photographs!" she demanded.

"I said I took them." He spaced his words out evenly.

What London said finally started to register. She tilted her head to the side, her forehead wrinkled with confusion. "*You* took them?" she asked.

"Yes."

"Why?"

London let out a sigh of pure frustration. "Believe it or not, I care about you."

Bianca looked up and something in the depth of his eyes made her heart skip a beat before she shook the feeling away. "Do you really think I am that stupid? Since when do you care about me?"

His brow rose in confusion. "We're friends. Why wouldn't I care about a friend?"

She dropped the envelope to the table and bore angry eyes into him. "Which one of them paid you to spy on me?" she demanded. "Was it Jaden or Jace?" He opened his mouth, but she held up her hand, cutting him off. "You would think since they have families, they'd have better things to do than to be meddling in my life. Damn them! Damn you!"

"I'm sorry. I didn't come over here to upset you."

A single tear slid down her cheek. "Well, you did!" she flopped back onto the couch. "Now what? Now that you've ruined my life, what's next? You go back and give your report?"

London's looks softened. "No. I'm not giving them anything. No one will know about this but you and me."

"Oh, boy, is that supposed to make me feel better!" She glanced down at the pictures of Collin in the arms of a beautiful woman and her stomach churned. Suddenly, she felt so nauseated she rose. "Oh, I'm going to be sick."

Before she made it halfway down the hall, London came up behind her, scooped her into his arms and carried her to the bathroom just in time. She emptied the contents of her stomach and when she was done, he handed her a cold wet towel so she could wipe her face. She rose to her feet and rinsed her mouth out, then leaned against the edge of the sink for strength.

"Finished?" he asked.

She nodded weakly and didn't object when he lifted her in his arms once again and carried her back into the living room, placed her on the sofa and sat beside her. Bianca closed her eyes and rested her head on his shoulder, waiting for her stomach to settle and her world to quit spinning.

Her fiancé was having an affair!

What was she going to do? Word had already gotten around that she was getting married. She hadn't been too happy about the gossip, but Collin seemed quite pleased about it. She dropped her forehead to her hands. "Oh, God, I'm going to be sick."

"You need me to carry you…"

Bianca placed a palm on London's chest and pushed against the solid muscles. "No, I just need for you to leave."

"I'm not leaving until I know that you're okay."

Uncontrollable tears were now running down her face. She swallowed. "How am I going to be okay when you just ruined my life?"

He looked confused by her response. "Ruined your life? I just saved you from a disaster."

Angrily, Bianca rose, desperate to put some distance between them. "Is that what you think you did?" She gave a stifled laugh. "Don't try to act like you care. The only reason you stuck your nose in my business is because Jaden paid you to do so."

"You should be happy," he said with utter seriousness.

"Happy? Happy? Why would I be happy?" Her eyes misted. "Everyone in Sheraton Beach knows I'm supposed to get married and now I need to figure out what to do."

London rose in one fluid motion. "What is there to think about? Those pictures should be all you need to know. He doesn't deserve you."

"Just go away. I need to think." She moved over to the love seat, sat down and buried her face in her hands. "Dear God, what have you done? My mother is going to have a cow when she finds out," she added miserably. "Just go away and leave me alone."

She was going to be the laughingstock of their stupid little town. All because London stuck his nose in her business. For the longest time she sat there with her legs folded beneath her, with her head on the armrest and her hands covering her face, as the images of Collin and the other woman kept flashing before her face. She didn't need to see the photographs again because they would forever be emblazoned in her mind.

"What am I going to do?" she mumbled, then looked up to find London still standing there, staring at her like an idiot. "I thought I told you to leave."

"Bianca, he isn't worth it," was his smooth reply.

"No, he isn't," she began with a sob in her throat. "But it's a little too late for that now."

"Why…what's wrong?"

"If you must know…I'm pregnant."

Chapter 7

*P*regnant.

No, he couldn't have possibly heard her right.

"Did you say you're pregnant?"

Pulling herself up to her full five-foot-two-inch height, Bianca frowned. "Yes, I said I'm pregnant. Now go and tell Jaden and let me sit here and feel sorry for myself." She moved over to the window with her arms folded against her chest, as if she were suddenly cold. Closing her eyes, she murmured, "My mother is going to kill me."

London couldn't have been more stunned if she had suddenly reached out and punched him hard in the stomach. *Pregnant.* "Your mother can be a little over the top at times, but I think she'll get over it eventually."

"Eventually?" she mocked, then snorted rudely. "She's never going to forgive me for this. Especially not after everyone finds out Collin was messing around on his pregnant fiancée with another woman. All my mother cares about is how things look. And this looks like something on one of those daytime soap operas. Oh, God! I'll never hear the end of it."

He hated to admit it, but Bianca was right about that. In a town as small as Sheraton Beach, everybody knew everybody and gossip was rampant. This would be the scandal of the year.

London knew Bianca was in pain and something inside tugged at his gut and told him to do or say something comforting. "How did you…"

She swung around. "Get pregnant? I guess I represent condoms' two percent failure rate." Moving away from the window, she added, "It must have happened two months ago when I suspected that one had broken." She flopped down on the couch. "How could Collin do this to me? I thought he loved me!" she shouted, then started crying again. She looked so miserable London closed his eyes and silently cursed Jaden under his breath for getting him involved in Bianca's personal life.

He was tempted to apologize, say his goodbyes and start walking, but Bianca was hurting. Considering the evidence before her, she had every right to be devastated. No matter what he personally thought of the creep, Bianca obviously loved Collin. She wouldn't have been engaged to him otherwise. He couldn't expect her to simply brush it off, chalk it up as a loss and get over the betrayal in a matter of minutes.

He moved over to the side of the couch and knelt down in front of her. He never liked to see a woman cry. Only he didn't know what to say or do. He reached for the box of tissues on the end table and handed it to her. When Bianca noticed his kind gesture, she broke down and sobbed openly.

Immediately, London scooped her up into his arms and took a seat on the couch cradling her against his chest while she cried. He tried to ignore the feelings she aroused in him as he held her sweet, soft body against him. She felt so good in his arms, he found himself tightening his hold with one hand while he stroked her cheek with the other.

"Everything's going to be okay," he whispered words of reassurance close to her ear. "It will all work out—just wait and see."

He'd forgotten how delicately Bianca was built. She seemed so small, with her shoulders slumped in resignation and her body curled in a ball across his lap.

"You're not in this alone. I know your family would never turn their backs on you."

She raised her eyes to his. They were so close he could see a tiny mole on the side of her delectable mouth that he had never noticed before.

"I know my family means well and they would do everything in their power to support me…after the initial shock," Bianca began between sniffles. "Mother will cry, the three J's will start in on how they taught me better than that, and then they'll be out hunting for Collin. And there is no telling what they'll do once they find him." She paused for a long thoughtful moment. "Even though that doesn't sound like a bad idea." Realizing that she was being ridiculous, she shook her head. "Then there are the towns-people and the gossiping. Mother would lock herself in the house for weeks and you know how she loves to shop. I'm sorry, but I can't bring that kind of scandal to my family. Having a baby out of wedlock is unacceptable and you know it. No woman in my family has ever found herself pregnant without a husband. We Beaumont women have too much common sense to let some-thing like that happen…until now." She sniffled. "Why can't the floor just open up and swallow me?"

He felt sorry for her because he knew that everyone in the town looked up to the Beaumont family as if they were role models. One slipup and they would never hear the end of it. Bianca was right. The second they caught wind that she was pregnant, and the father was nowhere around, her family would start feeling the heat.

"How far along are you?"

Despair swept over her face. "Almost three months."

London pulled back and made sure she saw the incredulous look on his face. "Three months! And you haven't said anything?"

Feeling a little flustered, she batted his arm away then moved and took the seat on the couch beside him.

"I've only known for a few weeks. I was so busy working on the marketing campaign for the new hotel that I didn't even notice when I'd missed my period."

"Didn't you have morning sickness?"

"A little." Bianca dragged her knees to her chest and rested her chin on her knees. "I thought it was stress. Collin was worried about his unit being deployed and I guess in the back of my mind I was worried about that, too. Then he started asking me to marry him and as much as I wanted to, I just wasn't sure if I really…" she dropped her voice and cleared her throat as if she suddenly remembered who it was she was sharing her personal life with.

"What made you finally decide to agree to marry him?"

She didn't meet his eyes and the answer became obvious. He nodded knowingly. "When you found out you were pregnant." It wasn't a question, even though she nodded at his statement.

His lips pressed into a grim line. "Does he know that the baby is the only reason why you agreed?"

Slowly, she shook her head. "He doesn't know I'm pregnant."

London wiped a hand down his face. "This is great, Bianca, just great! Why the hell didn't you tell him?"

She hitched her chin high as she pointed down at the photographs. "Considering the evidence, do you really think that would have made a difference?" she barked sarcastically. Taking a deep breath, she added, "I had planned to surprise him on our honeymoon."

There was a long, strained silence. "So what are you going to do now?"

"Not that it's any of your business, but I plan to keep the baby. I'll just have to raise her myself." She rose and moved over to the love seat, putting distance between them, and he was grateful. Her sweet scent was driving him crazy.

She was right. It didn't concern him. But he'd seen too many women struggle to raise children on their own. He knew she would never have to worry about money, but the thought of her going through the pregnancy alone, not to mention raising a child without a husband bothered him. Her baby didn't deserve to be the subject of gossip.

"What about Collin? He does have a right to know about his child."

She snorted rudely. "Just as I had a right to know he was messing around on me! I don't want to have anything to do with him ever again, and neither will my child."

He stared across and witnessed the anger burning in the depths of her eyes. This was the Bianca he knew, the independent woman who didn't let anything or anyone stand in her way.

"I think raising your child alone would be a mistake," he said finally. "A child needs a father." She didn't respond. "Bianca, I've been out in the real world. And a woman can't teach a boy how to be a man."

Bianca met his gaze again and her walnut eyes were troubled. He sensed that she wasn't very confident about raising a child alone.

"That's what I've got three brothers for. Lord, I feel sorry for this baby if I'm having a girl. The three J's won't let a boy come within twenty feet of her." Despite her despair, she giggled, then suddenly stopped, struggling with her emotions. "I can do this. I know I can. I love kids and I've always wanted a family of my own. It's not quite the way I had planned it, but it will work out."

London began to pace. He'd never seen this side of Bianca. He assumed that she was perfectly happy with her demanding job and her friends and her many charitable activities. He knew she read children's books to students at the local elementary school, but he never guessed that her motherly instincts had kicked in.

"If that's your choice, then I support you one hundred percent," he said after a moment, "but before you make your final decision I want you to think about what you'll be doing."

Her temper flared without warning. "London, I'm not getting rid of my baby!"

He looked at her and felt a sense of relief to know that she already cared about the little life growing inside her. "Good. I'm glad. I just want you to be sure you realize what you're up against. I know you're having a hard enough time worrying about your parents' reaction."

"Yes, but I'm keeping this baby even if they threaten to disown me. I've saved enough money that I can get by for a while."

Not to mention the trust fund her grandfather had left each of the Beaumont children and grandchildren. Rumor had it that Roger Beaumont Sr. had left them millions. No, money was not an issue for any of them.

"So what's the next step?"

"I don't know. I was thinking of maybe taking an extended

vacation and moving out of the country for the next six months."
She gave a strangled laugh.

"Ha-ha. Nice try." He moved back over to the couch with one
hand tucked in the front pocket of his pants.

She sobered then leaned her head back against the cushion
and he watched the worry return to the corners of her mouth and
eyes. "I just wish it didn't matter so much what other people
think of me."

He shrugged. "You care about other people's feelings and
there's nothing wrong with that."

Bianca pushed her hair back from her face. "Yes, there is,
when it affects a decision I have to make about my life. I should
be excited about this baby growing inside me; instead all I can
think about is how much I'm disappointing my parents."

"I really think you should try talking to them."

She frowned.

"What about your brothers?"

This time she shook her head. "Absolutely not."

"Then you're going to have to come up with a plan. I don't
know much about having babies, but I do know that it's not too
much longer before you'll start showing."

"The only reason I was marrying Collin was because I was
carrying his child."

His brow rose. "You don't love him?"

"No, not really. Seeing those pictures, I realized that I am
more humiliated than heartbroken. I suspected my feelings for
him weren't that strong, but in order to have a father for my child
I was willing to give us a chance. Don't get me wrong. I am quite
fond of Collin, and he is a very caring and compassionate person,
but there was something missing in our relationship." Her eyes
rose to meet his. "But I guess that's no longer important."

"Nope. I guess it's not." He gave her a warm smile. "If you
like, I can go with you to talk to your parents."

"Thanks, that's sweet of you but this is something I have to
figure out on my own." Momentarily, Bianca closed her eyes
again and he watched her lower lip tremble. She wasn't as confident as she tried to make him believe. "I wish there were some
way I could rent a husband for nine months."

He chuckled and Bianca opened her eyes, smiled and laughed along with him.

"Sure you can. You'll just have to find someone else to marry you."

Bianca suddenly stopped laughing and her eyes grew large with astonishment. "Oh, my goodness! London that's a wonderful idea. If I can find someone else to be my fiancé, my parents will never know the difference. You wouldn't know anyone stupid enough to want to do that, would you?"

"Yeah, actually, I do. What's wrong with me?"

Chapter 8

The words were out of London's mouth before he realized it. *Now what had made him go and say something like that?* he wondered. Guilt probably. What else could it have been? The last thing he needed in his life was a pregnant woman on the rebound. Especially one he was attracted to.

Bianca was staring at him suspiciously. He raised his eyebrows questioningly.

"You don't think that you and I should—that we would…" pausing, she shook her head and gave a half laugh. "No, of course not." She gave another laugh. "London, you can be a clown when you want to be."

Insulted, London frowned at her. He hadn't meant to volunteer to help her, but now that he had he wondered what was so funny about his proposal.

Bianca didn't wait for his reply. She rose and headed into the kitchen. Pride refused to let his suggestion go unanswered.

Following her, he stepped into the spacious kitchen to find Bianca pulling out a box of decaffeinated tea from the cabinet.

"What do you mean, of course not?" he asked as he moved and rested his elbows against the granite countertop.

"Forget, I even said that." She laughed with a shake of her head, as if the idea were completely ridiculous, he noted with mounting annoyance. "I didn't mean to laugh but I know you're not even trying to go there with me." She dropped a tea bag in the mug, then filled it with fresh tap water.

Folding massive hands over a broad chest, London glared over at her. "And why not?"

Her eyebrows rose slightly as if she were surprised that he'd even ask.

"Why…because…well…" And then she burst out laughing.

London felt his indignation grow. Marriage was the last thing on his mind, yet here he was trying to help her and she had the nerve to laugh at his offer. Fine, he didn't want to get married, anyway, or did he? No, of course not, yet he felt somewhat responsible for ruining her engagement, although, as far as he was concerned, he had saved her from a disaster.

It wasn't a totally ridiculous idea. Getting married was not a bad idea at all. It could be a business arrangement. People did that all the time. Bianca, however, did not seem to see the sense in it. Bianca needed a husband, yet she laughed at the idea of marrying him. He tilted his chin stubbornly. Almost every single woman in Sheraton Beach was throwing herself at him, hoping to catch his attention. "Because of *what?*"

Bianca's laughter died away slowly as she suddenly realized that he wasn't joking. "Because we aren't right for each other," she said. "You're a…" He raised an eyebrow at her hesitation and she sighed. "You didn't mean it, did you?"

His silence was her only answer.

Bianca noticed the sober expression on his face and stared wordlessly across the room, almost certain that her expression mirrored her shock. His proposal had caught her completely by surprise. Never in a million years would she have expected him to offer to marry her. Was he for real?

Bianca gazed over at him, taking in the stubborn set of his eyes and his handsome features—a stubborn jaw, a sensual lower lip. Fitted together, it was an attractive package. Very attractive. She swallowed as she found her body responding to the possibilities. There was no way she could be married to him and not be tempted to…

"You can't be serious."

When she finally turned her gaze back to meet his eyes, he eyed her warily and waited. "I wouldn't have asked you if I wasn't serious."

Pulling her thoughts together, she gave him a critical squint. "You and I wouldn't last twenty-four hours and you know it."

"Why not?" Those two words were layered with a thread of annoyance.

She gave him a dismissive wave as she carried her mug over to the microwave, stuck it inside and set the timer. "I'm too independent and strong-minded. If I'm going to agree to an arranged marriage, it needs to be with a man who's going to leave me alone for the next six months. Not to mention sleep in the spare bedroom."

"Not happening," he snapped. "No real man would even consider that. If you're my wife, I plan to be your husband, which means you would be sharing my bed."

Her stomach churned at the possibility. At the heat in his eyes, she quickly turned away. "No way. I will never give my heart to another man."

"I didn't say anything about your heart."

Bianca swallowed at the intensity of his gaze. And wondered why on earth he was making this discussion so difficult. "I do not wish to marry a man unless he understands that it is strictly a business arrangement. I'll even pay him if I have to. The marriage would be in name only. He sleeps in one room and me in the other."

London chuckled. "He is not going to agree to that."

"For the right price he will."

She turned and he couldn't speak from staring. Through her snug T-shirt, he could see her body was already changing. Studying her carefully, he realized that her small breasts were fuller and more generous. Now that she was pregnant, he bet he could fit one in the palm of his hand.

Within seconds, his body betrayed him. Bianca was the best thing he'd ever laid eyes on. Staring at her, desire hardened the flesh pulsing between his thighs. London forced his gaze back up to her face, lingering on the tempting curve of her lower lip before returning to her mesmerizing walnut-colored eyes. He couldn't speak, so instead he drank in the sight of her.

Bianca was oblivious to him as she fussed with the sugar bowl. Finally, the bell on the microwave went off and she carefully removed her mug. "London?"

"Huh?"

"You weren't really serious about getting married, were you?"

He clamped his teeth together and forced a deep breath. "Yes, I am," he replied after recovering his voice.

A smile trembled on her lips. She was clearly surprised and flattered by his offer. Even if it was for all the wrong reasons. "You just feel sorry for me."

He gave a snort. "Feel sorry for you?"

"Because I'm pregnant by a jerk."

Feeling more at ease, London crossed his ankles, and leaned back against the counter. "Bianca, my offer of marriage was sincere. Feeling sorry for you is the last thing you would ever allow a man to feel. You're too strong a woman for that. I am confident that everything will work out for you." He waved her worries aside. "You are one of the most headstrong women I have ever met. You're definitely no pushover. I'm simply offering you a solution. Not because I think you need help caring for your baby, but because I know how important it is to you to protect your baby and your family from scandal."

Capturing her questioning gaze and holding it with his, he continued, "I know this is not at all how you had it planned, but you're in a bind and I think this arrangement could work if you'd let it. We can get married and live together until the baby is born. Once you're settled, you could file for a divorce. Hell, I'll even say it was my fault that our marriage didn't work."

Bianca's heart wrenched as she considered what he offered. Lowering her head slightly, she took a deep calming breath. The playboy was not at all father material, but she was certainly grateful for London's willingness to help her.

A tense silence enveloped the room. London was the first to say something.

"So what do you say, Bianca?"

As he spoke her name, it became a caress, one that sent shivers of warning down her spine. She looked up again and blushed profusely when she caught him staring. She half turned, stood there for a moment, utterly speechless as the room seemed to shrink in size. It reminded her of when she was seventeen and she thought she was madly in love with him. Back then, London only had eyes for Tiffany Spires. Now, his steady gaze was focused intently on her. She shivered. Realizing that she was holding her breath, she exhaled and hot air gushed from her lungs.

Bianca drew herself up sharply. This would not do, it simply would not do. London was a friend of hers and she was supposed to be in love with another man. Of course, she was still feeling the sting of Collin's betrayal. That was the only excuse she had for feeling this…this vulnerable. It didn't help that London was staring at her with hunger burning from the depths of his eyes. Her skin heated, and she was tempted to order him out of her kitchen and push him out the front door. Besides, it wouldn't work between them. London Brown loved women and she had sense enough to know there was no way he could stay committed to her for a year without feeling tempted to mess around. Then she would be back at square one, right where she started. If that was the case, she might as well just marry Collin. At least no one around here knew him or his reputation. But then there was that determined look in London's eyes that told her that London was a man of his word and that was what almost made her almost willing to take a chance. Having him by her side would make dealing with her parents so much easier. The only problem was that there was no way she could protect her heart for that long a time. She had run away from him before, but if she agreed to marry him there was no way she would be able to control her feelings, especially now that she was pregnant and her hormones were all out of whack.

As if he knew that she was considering his offer, London closed the distance between them and there was nowhere for her to go. Her eyes met his and held. She shivered uncontrollably, ripples of something she shouldn't feel for London shimmering through her body. He clasped her gently at the waist and pulled her into the circle of his arms. His breath was so close to her nose that his lips actually brushed it. She was stunned speechless.

"We would be good together," he said as he backed her hips against the counter.

Her mind unable to actually grasp what he had said, she leaned into him, her breasts rising and falling quickly. "I...uh." She then gasped in surprise as his lips closed on the rim of her ear. He held on to her waist while he did some erotic things to her earlobe that made her turn into pudding in his hands. Moaning, mindlessly, she let her head drop limply back.

She arched against his body, her breasts pushing against the thin fabric of her T-shirt. When his mouth covered hers and his tongue slid out to trace her lips, she willingly opened for him. She suddenly came alive in his arms, a hungry groan slipping from her mouth while his strong hands moved up and down her spine curving her to conform to his own body. With him so close, there was no mistaking the hard, rigid length of him pressed against her.

"What are you doing?"

"Showing you how serious I really am."

He tasted so good she didn't want the kiss to end. One hand remained flat against the small of her back, arching her against him, while the other slid up to her neck, his fingers burrowing into the soft thickness of her hair.

Abruptly, London drew back and she stared up at him. There was no mistaking the hunger in his eyes. It shook her to the core. He gave her a few seconds to object before he leaned forward and took possession of her mouth once more. Bianca stiffened defensively, not daring to move. Stubbornly, she tried to stay in control and she refused to return his kiss. The pad of his thumb caressed the vulnerable flesh of her neck, and a small betraying shudder of reaction trembled through her entire body.

A sigh escaped her lips and she no longer had the desire to fight the moment. Giving in, she wrapped her arms around his neck, and allowed London to devour her mouth with a passion that stole all her breath and left her panting. The sudden fierce sexual thrust of his tongue against hers brought her up intimately against him, her breath escaping on a soft shiver of pleasure.

She wasn't quite sure what he was doing, but she didn't seem to be able to find the presence of mind to care. All that mattered was how good he made her feel and she hardly noticed as his hands inched their way beneath her T-shirt. When London's thumb grazed her nipple with deliberate emphasis, she gasped while her body quivered.

"What's wrong?" he whispered. "You like me playing with your nipples. Yes? No?" As he was whispering to her, London's hand moved over and found her other breast.

Bianca gasped as London plucked at one and again the other. It was like some sort of madness. He wasn't what she wanted or needed, and yet she wanted and needed him with a violence that would have scared her, had she seen it coming.

Then suddenly London released her.

Blinking, Bianca opened her eyes, her chest heaving with her gasps as she saw London back away with his hands buried in his pockets as he, too, struggled for air. The look in his eyes told her that he had felt the same intensity.

"I just thought I'd leave you with something to think about," he said with a wink and a victorious smile. London then turned on his heels and headed out the front door.

Chapter 9

London pulled away from the curb and blew out a long, frustrated breath. To be totally honest, he had been a little offended at her for laughing at his offer. He was simply trying to do her a favor. Save her the embarrassment of the town finding out about her dilemma.

Turning the corner, he let out a harsh laugh. He could have anyone he wanted, but he ran away from any woman who even hinted at love and marriage. Glancing up into the rearview mirror, he tilted his chin proudly. He was one of the most eligible bachelors in Sheraton Beach, and he preferred to keep it that way. The last thing he needed was a wife and a child. As he thought about the mess he got himself into, he squeezed the steering wheel until his knuckles turned white. He had to force himself to loosen his grip.

As he drew closer to his house, he decided that he had to have his head examined. He had just asked his best friend's sister to marry him. *And she turned you down.* Maybe it was a good thing that she'd rejected his offer, because the three J's would have found out and he would have a lot of explaining to do.

Five minutes later, he pulled into his two-car garage and got out. As he stepped into his comfortable, three-bedroom house, he looked around. *Did he really want to give up his life?* he wondered.

Why are you worried about it? Bianca rejected your offer, so relax.

He couldn't relax—not as long as he knew he was responsible for ruining Bianca's evening. Before he had showed up at her door, she was planning to marry her baby's father. Now, after he had shoved the manila envelope in her face, her entire future was uncertain. And it was all his fault.

The cell phone rang and London reached inside his pocket and took it out. He looked down to see who was calling and swore under his breath.

Tracina.

Damn, he was supposed to be at her house, in her bed an hour ago.

"Hey, Tracina."

"London, sweetie, where are you? I'm lying here waiting on you."

He blew out a deep breath. The carefree life of a bachelor. Did he really want to give that up? He took a moment to think about that and all he could see was Bianca looking so small and all alone curled up on the couch. He'd had a lot of women in his life, but never had a female's femininity cried out to his manhood the way Bianca's had. For some strange reason, her being pregnant made him want her more than anything.

"I can't tonight. Something's come up."

"Anything I can do to help change your mind?" she purred.

London groaned as he thought about what he was giving up tonight. Tracina had the most magical hands.

"No, it's something that I have to take care of myself. Can I get a rain check?"

"Absolutely."

London hung up the phone, then ran a frustrated hand down his face. Bianca was definitively going to be the death of him.

But he was a man of his word and his offer still stood. He would give her some time to think about the two of them together and until he heard from her, he would just have to put his personal life on hold.

He tried to envision Tracina lying naked across her large poster bed, but all he could see was Bianca's wide eyes staring up him.

Damn, I need my head examined.

He walked up to his room and sat on the end of the bed. And found himself wondering about the two of them sharing his home, his bed. Knowing Bianca, she would want something bigger and better. She was born into money, while he had to work hard for everything he had. His family restaurant was a result of three generations of long hours and hard work, and it could all be taken away with the strike of a match if he wasn't smart, not to mention, careful. Fortunately for him, he had learned how to invest his money and over the years he had accumulated a portfolio that would make even a Beaumont gasp. No one knew his net worth, and he preferred to keep it that way. He wanted a woman to be attracted to who he was, not what he had.

Closing his eyes, London could still taste Bianca on his tongue, and the memory sent everything male about him into overdrive. She was a stubborn woman, but he was a stubborn man. She needed him. She just didn't realize it yet.

He was willing to bide his time, then he would make his move. Patience had never been one of his strong suits. He would just have to show her how good they could be together.

Bianca needed a husband and that man was going to be him.

London had left her house over an hour ago, yet Bianca was still rooted in the same exact place. She couldn't believe that London had offered to marry her! She was already engaged, or at least she was until Collin returned home this evening. Just thinking about Collin caused her blood to boil.

To think she was pregnant by that two-timing loser. She must have been blinded by his good looks to have been so naive that she hadn't seen the signs. Whoever the woman was, it was obvious they knew each other quite well. The pictures were all dated over the last three days.

Reaching for her mug, she put the untouched tea back into the microwave. Now that London was gone, she could drink her tea in peace while she tried to clear her head and think about her next move.

The phone on the wall rang and she ignored it. She didn't have to look to know who it was. Collin. His phony plane had landed.

Tough luck. There would be no limousine picking him up tonight. He would just have to find his own way home. She would deal with him later. Right now she had more important things to worry about. Her unborn child.

Marry me.

Was he really serious? Nah, not London.

There was no way London was ready to give up his carefree lifestyle, even for her. Yet when she'd stared up into his eyes, her hands had trembled because what she saw told her that he was dead serious.

But married to London Brown? How in the world would she be able to keep her heart intact? As much as she hated to admit it, London was one of the finest men she knew, which didn't make resisting him easy.

While they had dated, there were several times she had considered taking him home to her bed and giving in to that chemistry she felt every time he was around.

Two things had stopped her. One was that London had a reputation as a player. She would have just been another notch on his bedpost. After he'd gotten what he'd wanted, the challenge of having her would have gone and so would London. The second reason was that there would have been no way for her to separate her heart from her body. She had to feel something for a man before she could even consider sleeping with him, and what she felt for London was too strong to be ignored for too long.

The timer went off and Bianca retrieved her rewarmed tea from the microwave oven. From the other room she could hear her cell phone ringing and again she let it go. Instead, she moved to the window over the sink and stared out into the dark, starlit night. Right about now she should be cussing, screaming and crying her eyes out because Collin was unfaithful. Instead, she felt angry and confused.

She placed a hand gently over her abdomen. "It's going to be okay, little one. Mama's not going to let anything happen to you," she whispered with assurance to her unborn child.

Days ago, she had come to the conclusion that getting

pregnant had been purely an accident. There was no point in beating herself up for getting pregnant by a no-good bastard. All she could do was push on and get ready to start a new life for her and her baby. What angered her most was that her baby would be without a father.

I want to be a father to your unborn child.

Even now his words caused her heart to lurch. She moved away from the window with a frustrated bark of laughter. She couldn't even think about considering his offer. Ridiculous, she thought, as she brought her mug to her lips.

The two of them, married. No way! It would never work and no one would ever believe it was a real marriage.

But despite her protest, heat settled down low at the thought of being his wife in every way.

Her mind raced back to when he had pulled her into his arms. Her entire body had turned into liquid fire. How could she have let her guard down, allowing her body to respond to him so brazenly? She had wanted his kisses. She had yearned for his hands on her breasts. Now London thought she was so desperate that she would allow him to do whatever he wanted. He thought she was so vulnerable that she was his for the asking.

But she wasn't and never would be. She knew that and she was going to make sure he knew it, as well.

She tilted her chin. She would do whatever it took to keep her family name out of the local gossip. She was determined not to make her parents look bad, she decided with renewed determination as she sipped her tea. She would find a way without getting married.

No matter how London made her feel, nothing could change the fact that she simply did not want an emotional or physical relationship with a man ever again. Collin had shown her that she could not trust men, and if Collin could not be trusted to mean it when he said that he loved her and wanted to marry her, then she certainly wasn't going to risk trusting a man like London Brown.

Chapter 10

"London did what?"

Bianca glanced around, reassuring herself that no one was listening. "Can you please keep it down?" Her tall, leggy friend had a habit of being a little too loud at times.

"I'm sorry," Debra said with an apologetic smile, then lowered her voice and said, "I can't believe it. The prince of chicken asked you to marry him."

"Very funny."

Debra chuckled. "I'm sorry. I don't know why I'm laughing because there are going to be a lot of haters when they find out that London Brown is about to come off the market."

"Wait a minute. I didn't say I was going to accept his proposal."

"Why not?"

Bianca pursed her lips at her. The answer should be obvious. "Because last week I was engaged to Collin. What will I look like telling everyone, 'Oops I made a mistake. I'm actually in love with London.'"

Debra pushed a blond curl out of her face and pierced Bianca with her green eyes hidden behind a pair of trendy glasses. "Are you in love with London?"

"Hell, no."

"My point exactly. No one knew the identity of your fiancé. Remember, you kept his identity a secret."

She had forgotten about that. "It doesn't matter. I'm still not even going to waste my time considering his offer. That man thinks he's God's gift to women."

"Yeah, but he chose you and that should say something," Debra replied, leaning toward her.

"All it says is that he feels sorry about taking those pictures and destroying what I had with Collin," she retorted with a dismissive wave of her hand.

Debra pointed a freshly manicured finger at her. "No, Collin did that on his own."

She was right. Collin had ruined everything. And the second his "imaginary" plane landed and she wasn't there greeting him with open arms, he caught a cab and rushed over to her house. She had already taped the photographs of him and his other woman to her front door. He saw them and spent the next half hour banging on her door, trying to explain until she finally called the police and told him never to call her again. A week had passed and Collin tried numerous times to get in touch with her before he'd finally gotten the hint. She hadn't heard from him in over a week. As disappointing as it was, their relationship was finally over.

"You have to admit, London is a good man to be willing to marry you and be the father of your child," Debra said on an envious sigh.

"It would only be a front long enough for me to have the baby and come up with a reason for us to divorce."

Debra pushed her glasses to the top of her head. "A lot can happen in that time."

Remembering the way her body had tingled when he kissed her caused a shiver to slide down her spine. "I doubt that. By then London will have grown restless and be ready to get back to being a playboy."

"And maybe not."

Sighing, Bianca met her gaze and asked, "Why are you so happy about the thought of me marrying him?"

"Because you know I've always liked him and he really is a good guy. It's not his fault that he looks good," she argued and laughed.

"Then why haven't you dated him?"

She turned up her nose. "That would be too much like dating one of my brothers."

Debra had five brothers, all older than her. That was something the two of them had in common—brothers. London went to school with Debra's youngest brother, Charles.

She didn't want to admit it, but she hadn't heard from London since he kissed her silent and then departed her house. Obviously, he wasn't serious about his offer because he hadn't called and was probably grateful that she had not called him, either.

"I still can't believe that Collin was messing around," Debra replied after swallowing a mouthful of potato salad. "Although I did tell you there was something about that man I didn't like. He went on too many deployments. I know the air force sends their people out on missions, but he was gone almost every weekend. Come on now."

Bianca nodded. She had had the same suspicions.

"At least you had sense enough to give him his walking papers." Debra reached across the table and gave her a high five.

"My mama ain't raised no fool. You know I don't believe in giving second chances. If he'd do it once, he'd do it again."

"Damn right," Debra said. "Did you tell him about the baby?"

"Nope."

Debra didn't look the least bit pleased by Bianca's answer. "Are you planning to tell him?"

Bianca released a heavy sigh of despair. "Maybe, eventually. He *is* the father of my child and he *does* have a right to know. I just won't tell him until after the baby is born." Pausing, she released a frustrated groan. "I wish I didn't have to deal with Collin. I have a hunch that when he finds out about the baby, he'll cause problems for me."

"Then what are you going to do?"

Bianca had been thinking about that all week and the only thing she was certain of was that she wasn't giving up her baby. "I always dreamed of having kids, but part of that fantasy

included a ring on my finger and a good man standing beside me."
Sighing, she added, "I'm just going to have to raise her myself."

Excitement shimmered in Debra's eyes. "It might be a boy."

She shook her head. "Uh-uh. This is a girl. We have enough boys in our family."

"That's for sure."

The waitress brought them both refills.

Bianca sobered and looked down into her iced tea. "I really want this baby. But what am I going to do when the whole town finds out that I'm having a baby out of wedlock?"

Debra frowned. "This isn't the fifties. Women have babies by themselves all the time."

She wished she had her friend's confidence.

"When are you planning to tell your parents?"

With a frustrated groan, Bianca dropped her head against the bench and stared up at the ceiling. They were the problem. The last thing the family needed was a scandal. And the Beaumont daughter being jilted and knocked up by her fiancé would be the talk of the town.

Suddenly, she lost her appetite. She could just see herself having that conversation with her parents. They would look at her with disappointment and shame. All her parents cared about was how things looked. And having a daughter pregnant and unmarried would be an embarrassment to the Beaumont name. Her mother was never going to forgive her.

Bianca looked over at her friend and saw the sympathy in her eyes and shook her head. "I don't know."

"You can't keep it a secret. At some point you're going to starting showing."

Blowing out a breath, she nodded and said, "Yes, I know."

Debra was right. The whole thing with her keeping her fiancé/baby's daddy a secret had gone on long enough. Soon, she promised, soon she would go to her parents' house and drop the bomb in their laps. Then she could go hide her head under the sand for the next six months until the baby was born.

"I guarantee that when your parents see that beautiful little baby they will get over it," Debra replied with a confidence Bianca wished she felt.

"Maybe, but what about the rest of the town?"

"Forget these nosy folks around here."

Bianca reached for her glass and was just about to take a sip when she felt a powerful stir. She looked over at the door and her gaze locked onto London's. Her heart did a somersault and landed somewhere low in her stomach. Damn, he made her nervous, but boy did he look good. He moved across the polished floor in dark blue jeans that hung low on his waist and a green-and-white short-sleeved, button-down shirt. He looked sexy and downright lethal.

"Hello, ladies." He stopped in front of their booth and reached over and gave Bianca's shoulder a gentle squeeze. His long fingers sent tingling shards of awareness through her body. Dammit! She couldn't concentrate with him standing that close.

"Hello, London. Come and have a seat next to me." Without waiting for an answer, Debra slid across the seat and patted the space beside her.

He lowered himself onto the bench, and Bianca swallowed the lump in her throat. He was sitting directly across from her. Their eyes met and she felt uneasy underneath his intense gaze. London smiled that enticingly sexy smile that always made her want to go with him to the nearest bedroom and satisfy her curiosity.

"How are you, Bianca?" he said, breaking into her wayward thoughts.

She blinked twice and returned to the present. "Well, let's see," she began, "my fiancé is a two-timer and I'm twelve weeks' pregnant, but other than that everything is peaches and cream."

"Everything would be if you'd accept my offer." He covered her hands with his and gave her a long, serious look.

Ms. Dramatic started fanning herself. "Ooh-wee! Girl, you'd better take him up on his offer. I've never see London this determined before."

With a roll of the eyes, Bianca pulled her hand away. "His offer is ridiculous and he knows it."

"It's no more ridiculous than your trying to raise a baby all by yourself."

"Women do it all the time," Bianca challenged.

"Yes, but they don't live in Sheraton Beach, nor is their last name Beaumont."

He did have a point, Bianca thought.

"Wait until your mother finds out," he added.

"I know that's right," Debra mumbled under her breath.

Bianca groaned inwardly. Why did he have to remind her? "You know, we were having a really good time until you showed up. Don't you have something else to do, like meddle in someone else's life?"

"I guess I deserved that one." He chuckled and didn't seem the slightest bit intimidated by her comment. "Debra asked me to join you." Bianca looked over at her best friend, who gave her an innocent look.

"I want the two of you to talk," Debra said.

"There isn't anything to talk about," Bianca replied then reached for her fork. "Besides this is not the type of conversation I want to have in public," she said stubbornly, then took a forkful of her macaroni. The smell of fish at the next table threatened to make her sick. She lowered her fork, reached for a napkin and spit the food out. Quickly, Debra reached over and gave her a plastic cup. With one hand over her stomach, Bianca stared across the table. "What am I going to do with that?" she asked with a ridiculous laugh.

Debra gave her a sheepish grin. "I thought you were about to throw up."

"And you thought I'd use this itty bitty cup?" she asked, then chuckled despite the queasiness of her stomach. "Yeah, right."

London moved around the table and slid onto the seat beside her. "Are you still having problems keeping food down?"

She nodded and tried to ignore the smell of his cologne. The light musky scent didn't bother her at all. She blamed the way her pulse was racing on the virile man alone. The last thing she needed was to get sick in the restaurant. "Yes, but the doctor said it should pass soon."

"Let me get you some crackers," he offered and before she could stop him, London rose and walked over to the counter.

As soon as he was out of earshot, Debra leaned across the table and slapped Bianca on the arm. "Girl, you'd better marry that man. Look at how attentive he is!"

Bianca answered with a rude snort. "Puhleeze, he just feels

guilty for screwing up my life. If he hadn't meddled, I wouldn't be thinking about being a single parent."

"No, instead you would have been marrying a two-timer."

"Yeah, I know." She knew she couldn't blame London, because it wasn't his fault. Not really. But as long as she continued to blame him for ruining her life, it made it easier to stay mad at him. "I need somebody to blame."

"Then blame Collin. I don't see him here trying to track down saltine crackers for you."

Bianca stared at Debra over the top of her eyes and despite her dilemma she couldn't help giggling. Her life was a mess. It was either laugh or cry because the whole thing was too ridiculous for words.

London returned with a small plate of saltine crackers. "Here, try these. I even got you some club soda to settle your stomach."

She glanced up at him towering over her and saw genuine concern. "Thanks, London."

His lips threatened to smile. "You're welcome." He returned to his seat next to Debra.

Bianca reached for a cracker, then paused and stared across the table at London for a long intense moment. He leaned back in his chair and continued to watch her.

"Look, I need to know something. Why would you want to help me?"

"Because I like you, why else?"

"Do you always offer to marry women you like?"

His eyes twinkled. "Only the pregnant ones."

She couldn't resist a smile, then tore her eyes away, ignoring the pounding of her heart.

Debra was grinning from ear to ear. "I think the two of you will be great together."

Bianca didn't agree. "Don't you want to marry a woman you really love?"

He gave her a long, thoughtful look before answering. "Maybe one day I'll meet a woman who makes my heart beat faster and who'll cry when I ask her to share the rest of my life with me, but until then I'm available to help a friend. The same goes for you. I'm sure some day you'll meet a really nice guy and fall in love. Just because your fiancé was a jerk doesn't mean the right man isn't out there for you."

She disagreed. "I think there is someone out there for everyone, my brothers' wives and my parents' forty-year marriage is proof of that. But for some reason I have a history of picking the wrong men and that's why I don't intend to ever allow myself to fall in love again. But that doesn't mean I don't believe marriage can work. It just doesn't work for me."

"Because…"

"Because it means giving my heart, and I'm not willing to do that again."

"It's too soon to say that."

Bianca shook her head. "No, it's not."

"That's too bad if you think sex will be enough," he said, as if he were challenging her. Sex was one path she did not want to go down with him. Just thinking about having him in her bed caused a warm deep sensation to pool down low.

London rose. "I'd better get back to the restaurant. I just wanted to stop in and see why the two of you were eating across the street at the competition." He winked, then strolled out the same way he'd come in.

Bianca nibbled on a cracker and watched as he crossed the wide cobblestone street and stepped inside his restaurant. When her eyes shifted, she noticed Debra shaking her head.

"What's wrong?"

"You, if you pass up a good thing like that. Hell, if I were in your shoes I'd be giving him my heart and a permanent place in my bed."

She broke off a tiny piece of cracker, lifted it to her lips and said, "I think we need to eat and get out of here."

"Okay, ignore me if you want to, but I saw the way the two of you were looking at each other. And that was more than friendship passing between you. I saw attraction and strong sexual chemistry. You're just too stubborn to admit it."

"I am *not* stubborn," she denied.

Debra rolled her eyes. "Yes, you are. You know I'm your girl, so I'm not going to lie to you. You have a tendency to want things your way."

Bianca lifted a brow. "And what's wrong with that?"

"Everything, when you're too blind to see what's standing right smack in front of your face. Or, in your case, what just walked across the street."

She gave an impatient sigh. "And what's that?"

"The answer to your problems."

Debra was wrong. Giving in to her feelings would stir up a whole new barrel of problems. Her attraction to London was something she could deny for only so long before she'd weaken and give in to him. And that would be a disaster. He was definitely a player, hardly husband material.

She was pulled from her thoughts when Debra slapped her across the arm. "Earth to Bianca."

"I'm listening."

"I asked you what your parents are going to say when you don't bring Collin to dinner with you tomorrow."

"Oh, no! I forgot that tomorrow is Thursday."

"Yep, and you've been making excuses long enough. They're going to know something is up."

"I guess I'm going to have to tell them the truth. They'll be relieved to know the engagement is off."

"Yeah, but what are they going to say to, 'Oh, by the way, I'm pregnant.'"

Now that *was the real problem.* A cracker lodged in her throat and Bianca reached for her glass of club soda, hoping to wash it down, then took a deep breath. All she could do was pray that her mother didn't have a fit.

Chapter 11

Jessica Beaumont waited until the table had been clear and coffee had been served to ask the question that she had been anxious to ask all evening. "When are we going to meet your fiancé?"

The conversations at the table ceased. All eyes were again on Bianca. She closed her eyes and gave a silent groan before looking at her mother again.

She brought her cup to her lips, sipped and sipped again. Stalling. The look on her mother's face said she'd had enough. "Maybe next week."

"You said that last week."

"He's been out of town."

Her mother's lips formed a disapproving line. "He can't possibly be out of town every week. What kind of life will the two of you have if he's never around?"

Bianca lowered her gaze to the slim gold watch on her wrist. "He's in the military, Mother. I'll bring him next week."

"Really?" Her tone said she didn't believe Bianca for a minute.

Jaden rose from the table. "I'm starting to think that your fiancé is make-believe."

Bianca rolled her eyes over in his direction. "If you thought that, then you wouldn't have paid London to spy on me," she spat. She saw the surprise register in his eyes.

After a long, tense moment, he finally replied, "I only did that because I care about you."

"Whatever. I'm tired of everyone trying to run my life," Bianca said angrily.

Luckily, Danica changed the subject when she announced the results of her second ultrasound. It was confirmed. They were having a little girl. The table exploded with excitement and, to Bianca's relief, she was out from under the microscope…for now.

After coffee, the family moved into the great room. Bianca edged her way to the door, hoping to make a quick escape. She had kissed her niece, rushed down the wide marble hallway, turned the knob on the door and was almost safely on the other side—

"Bianca."

Stopping dead in her tracks, she swore under her breath at the sound of a cultured voice coming from the living room. Bianca turned with a practiced smile. "Yes, Mother?"

Jessica shot her daughter a withering look. "Are you trying to sneak out while I'm not looking?"

Her shoulders sagged. There was really no point in lying. "Yes, Mother. I'm tired of your butting into my personal life."

Dramatically, Jessica brought a hand to her chest and gasped. "That's what mothers do…we worry about our children and want only the best for them. For Pete's sake! Can you at least tell me your fiancé's name?"

Bianca looked at her. Her eyes were steady. The grim determination of her mother's mouth said she wasn't backing down until she had answers.

"Okay," Bianca began and before she realized what she was doing, she took a deep breath and said, "His name is…London. London Brown."

Bianca parked her car in the driveway, slammed the door and headed up the drive. With each passing hour, she was sinking deeper and deeper into hot water. What in the world had she been thinking, telling her mother that she was engaged to London? She was almost certain her mother was already on the phone telling all her friends.

"Great, Bianca. Just great." Now she needed to do some damage control quickly before word got back to London. Wearily, she stuck her key into the lock. She was tired and needed to lie down for a few minutes, then she would change into jeans and a T-shirt and go see London, and tell him what happened before her mother told Jaden and then…all hell would break lose.

She unlocked the front door, stepped inside and went completely still when she spotted Collin reclining on her sofa. Her exhaustion was replaced with anger. "What are you doing here?" she said.

He rose and gave her his dimpled smile, while leaning his weight on one leg with his hands deep in his pockets. She knew him well enough to know that meant he wanted something. She was so determined to wipe that cocky smile from his face. She'd once found him attractive, with his bald head and dark brown eyes. Now she saw a man who was so manipulative, so full of crap she couldn't believe she had ever been attracted to him in the first place. How could she have been so stupid? So blind? And now she carried his child.

"How did you get in?"

Without breaking eye contact, he removed his hand from his pocket, and held up a ring that held a single key.

Bianca drew her head back and her eyes widened. She had never given him a key. One afternoon she had let him use her key to go back to her house and retrieve his laptop. He must have had a copy made. The smirk on his face told her he thought he was smarter than she was.

She shut the door behind her then crossed the room with determination. As soon as she neared him, she stuck out her hand and reached for the key, but Collin quickly stashed it back in his pocket.

"Give me my key," she demanded.

Instead of returning it, Collin reached out for her hand and held it. "Baby, please hear me out. I made a mistake. I love you and want to marry you."

Shock stopped her midstride. "What?"

"I love you. That woman meant nothing to me. She was

someone from my past. I was trying to find a way to break the relationship off without hurting her feelings."

He was so full of crap. She yanked her hand away. "You don't love me, Collin. It was all a big game to you. Please just give me my key and get out of my house. I've already given you back your ring—what more do you want?"

"You. I want to spend the rest of my life with you."

"The rest of our lives?" She crossed her arms and glared at him. "Now how in the world is that possible?"

She glimpsed a touch of panic before his gaze danced away and then returned. His throat worked as he swallowed. "Easy. I'm sorry. Why don't we go on our honeymoon to Alaska early. That way I can have ten days to show you how sorry I really am."

Bianca laughed loud enough to echo off the walls. She shook her head in disbelief. Did he really think she was that stupid? She'd rather eat dirt than be stuck ten days on a ship with him out in the middle of nowhere. She tilted her head back and gave him a menacing look. "You're full of crap."

"Come on, Bianca. Please believe me. What is it going to take for you to understand that I'm really sorry?"

Suddenly, Bianca felt an onslaught of nausea. She prayed it would dissipate. She placed a hand to her stomach then quickly removed it.

Collin eyed her suspiciously.

Hoping to throw off any suspicions he might be having, Bianca said, "I shouldn't have had that burrito at lunch." She moved over to the coffee table and dropped her purse. "Collin, our relationship is over. Go back to that woman you were playing house with."

He gave a strangled laugh. "Why would I want a broke woman when I can have you? Sweetheart, we will have a wonderful life together and never have to want for anything. That's the life I want."

Money. This was all about money. Why was she surprised? "You should have thought about that before you messed around on me. It's over."

"Sweetheart, what is it going to take for you to believe that I made a mistake? I'm sorry." He dropped down on one knee. "Please marry me."

"No."

"Bianca, baby," he singsonged. "Come on. We're good together."

Correction, before she had found out he was messing around, she was willing to make an exception. She had always had doubts about their relationship. There was no racing pulse or sweaty palms. Her heart didn't skip a beat when he was near. She didn't feel any of those things. In fact, if she weren't pregnant she would have ended the relationship sooner. She was only willing to give their relationship a shot for the sake of her baby, but that was before London had revealed his secret. "It's too late. Now leave before I call the police."

Anger flashed in Collin's eyes. He stalked to the door, turned the knob and opened it, but paused before stepping through and glared over his shoulder. "You're going to regret this," he warned. The door slammed behind him, causing Bianca to jump.

Her stomach revolted. She bolted to the bathroom and lost her dinner. When the retching ceased, she lowered to the floor and leaned back against the bathroom cabinet. What was she going to do? All Collin cared about was getting her money. There was no way she could let him get his hands on her baby.

She rested both hands on her stomach. She needed to get married before she started showing. Otherwise, Collin would know the baby was his.

Panic clawed at her insides.

Instantly, she rose from the floor, went into her bedroom and took a seat on the end of the bed. After reaching for the phone, she dialed his number. A sob slipped out of her throat when his deep baritone answered. "Hello?"

"London, I need you."

Chapter 12

London answered the door and Bianca walked in without waiting for an invitation. "Okay, if we're going to do this then you need to understand a few ground rules."

"I'm listening," he replied with a smile.

Bianca swung around to face him and her eyes widened. She had been in such a rush that she hadn't paid attention to what he was wearing, or, more precisely, what he wasn't wearing. She stared ahead at a beautifully milk-chocolate chest and a white towel, wrapped low on his hips. What she saw was enough to make a woman drool in appreciation.

You can do this. You can do this.

There was no way she was going to start wanting him. If they were going to be married, it was going to be strictly a business arrangement. She knew she needed to keep her eyes on his face, but she couldn't help noticing his flat stomach or the sprinkle of fine hair that traveled downward to where his towel had slipped slightly. Bianca swallowed, then took a deep breath. Oh, boy, maybe this wasn't such a good idea after all.

"If you keep on looking at me like that," he began in a low voice, "I might drop this towel and see where the moment leads us."

"I'm not looking at you," she said so quickly that London chuckled.

"Yes, you are. You're looking like you want me to sweep you up in my arms and carry you back to my room and finish what we started the other night."

Her stomach churned. "You've got such an imagination," she said with a nervous laugh. "And such a big head that you think everybody wants you. Guess what, I don't."

"So if I took this towel off right now, it wouldn't affect you in the slightest?" He said, then taunted her by hooking his thumbs inside the top of his towel.

She made a nonchalant shrug. "Not at all."

He loosened the towel and only seconds before revealing what was underneath, Bianca swung around—a cowardly motion—turning her back to him. "Wait! Keep your clothes on. Either you want to talk about your offer to help me or you don't."

He gave her a chuckle that said, Chicken. "Yeah, yeah, I'm listening."

Bianca took a deep breath. Glad that he had stopped when he had. Another few seconds of that and *she* would have been ripping the towel off, begging him to fill her with everything he had. Glad that her sanity had returned and her pulse slowed, she gave him a few seconds and when she was certain the coast was clear she swung around and this time focused on the area above his neck.

"Okay, let me hear your ground rules."

"If I agree to marry you, it will be in name only."

"Meaning?"

"Meaning we sleep in separate beds and no…you know…"

His brow rose in amusement. "You know, what?"

"You know?"

"Sex?"

She nodded.

He shot her a long hard look, then shook his head stubbornly. "Absolutely not. If we're going to marry, you are going to be my wife in every sense of the word."

She swallowed. "Meaning?"

"Meaning," London began as he took a step forward, "I want you to surrender all of you."

"You're kidding? Right?"

Again, he shook his head and said, "Nope."

Bianca was shaking and tingling at the same time. "Why, when this will be nothing more than a business arrangement?"

London shrugged and gave her a sly smile. "Hey, you got to give a little to get a little. Haven't you heard that saying before?"

"But we're not going to stay married that long!" She protested, determined to do whatever it took for him to understand that if the two of them were intimate, it would be a big mistake.

"It doesn't matter. I'm attracted to you and I know that you are attracted to me, as well." She opened her mouth to deny the obvious, but he held up a hand interrupting her. "Bianca, you know it's true, so I don't know why you keep trying to fight it."

"I'll admit that you're not bad looking."

"Not bad looking!" He had the nerve to look insulted before he started laughing. "I don't have to tell you that every available woman in Sheraton Beach wants me. Hell, even some of the married ones want me."

Her eyes rolled. "Then let them have you."

"They don't need my help. You do."

Damn him for reminding her of how desperate she was. She would have scouted around for someone else if she hadn't already told her mother that she was engaged to him.

"I just want to know…what is it about me that you're afraid of?"

"I'm not afraid of you," she lied, just as the telephone rang.

"Hold that thought," London replied, then moved over to the cordless phone on the table and answered it. "Hello, Dad." Whatever his father said caused London's eyebrows to shoot up. "Engaged? Who told you that?"

Uh-oh.

London continued to listen and Bianca felt the heat of his eyes when they came over to rest on her panic-stricken face. "Oh, really? Dad, let me give you a call back."

London hung up, then folded his arms against his chest. "Is there something you need to tell me?"

She was certain her cheeks had turned three shades of red. "Well, I kind of already told Mother that we were engaged."

He chuckled. He was getting a kick out of this. "Kind of, meaning what?"

He was going to make her say it. "Meaning, I told her at dinner tonight the name of the man I was engaged to."

"And that man just happened to be me?"

"Yes."

"Wow!" With a silly smirk on his face, he walked to an oversize leather recliner and had a seat. "So in other words, you need me now."

Damn the man. Bianca realized that he wasn't going to be happy until he had her squirming like a fish out of water. "Something like that," she murmured.

"But I thought you said it wouldn't work?"

Bianca released a heavy sigh of despair. How in the world had she gotten herself into this mess? "I guess it's better than the truth."

London paused to study her, then nodded and agreed. "Your mother must have called and told one of her friends because word has already gotten back to my father. His feelings are hurt that he had to hear about his son's engagement from the checker at the grocery store."

Bianca groaned inwardly. Somedays she hated living in such a small town. News definitely spread fast. "I'm sorry."

"You should be." He snaked out an arm and pulled her down onto his lap.

"Let me go!"

"Woman, hold still and give your fiancé a kiss!"

Bianca struggled until she freed herself, then rose and stood over him. London almost fell off the recliner, he was laughing so hard. The way the towel was shifting to the side was making her blood pressure rise.

"You are really getting a big kick out of this. Don't forget that it's all your fault."

"Yeah, yeah. I know," he said and suddenly got serious. "That's why I offered to marry you in the first place."

She didn't respond.

He rose. "I guess I'd better make this official." Then to her horror he dropped down on one knee in front of her.

"What…what in the world are you doing?"

London took her hand. "Proposing, the right way. Bianca Michelle Beaumont, will you marry me?"

Her heart was pounding rapidly. As she stared down at his sober expression, she felt her stomach quiver. She hadn't felt any of those things when Collin had proposed. And this time it wasn't even real! Somewhere deep inside, for several crazy seconds, she found herself wishing the proposal were the real thing.

"Are you gonna leave a 'brotha' hanging?"

Bianca gave him a smile and decided to play along. After all, he had offered to help her dodge a scandal. The least she could do was show her gratitude. Getting into character, she gasped, brought a hand to her chest and said, "Oh, my God! Yes, Yes! I'll marry you."

London dropped her hand and frowned. "Very funny."

"I thought so," she said and giggled.

She should have known that London was the type of man not to let her get away with trying to challenge his masculinity. He rose and she swallowed when she realized what he was about to do. Ignoring her shocked cry of protest, he moved against her and leaned forward. He had every intention of kissing her.

"I really don't think this is a good idea."

"I think it's a damn good idea," he said softly.

He took her breath away the moment his mouth came down on hers, and the jolt of awareness exploded through her whole body. When he parted her lips with the tip of his tongue, she was ready and opened completely for him. He tasted heavenly.

His left hand trailed the length of her body to her knee then slowly stroked up the inside of her thighs. Helplessly, she closed her eyes and gave in to his intimate touch.

"You like that don't you?"

"No," she moaned in outrage. He had no right touching her that way.

"Liar," he snarled. His hand moved across her body to her breast, shaping it then rubbing his thumb over the erect swell of her nipple until her body took over and reacted with a series of sensual shudders that raced through her.

"Tell me now if you want me to stop."

Don't.

Stop.

Don't stop.

His mouth was pleasuring her beyond anything she had ever known. He cupped the back of her head to bring their mouths closer, her hands reached up, she wrapped her arms around his neck urging him to continue the kiss forever. She took his tongue into her mouth, savored and connected with it. No man had ever kissed her this way before, and she knew that no man ever would kiss her this way again.

Suddenly, Bianca felt herself being swung up into his arms and placed on his lap as he continued to kiss her.

His hand dipped between her thighs, beneath her knit dress. Instinctively, she sucked in a gulp of air, waiting for the heat of his hand against her most intimate place. Sanity was long forgotten. Her traitorous body had taken over. With his fingers, he slipped past her panties and parted the lips of her sex, finding wetness waiting for him. She sucked in a breath. Oh, this is what she needed. He began to torture her with slow gentle strokes that made her body jerk. His tongue continued to move in and out of her mouth, matching the rhythm of his fingers. She grabbed on to his arm and held on for dear life. Soon she was whimpering and she cried out.

"I think you like it," he whispered, his lips closed to her ear.

"No…yes," she whispered, her words broken, incoherent. She didn't know what she was saying or thinking, and right now she didn't have time to care. She had far more important things to be thinking about.

Like what his fingers were doing.

She leaned into his touch and rocked with the rhythm of his fingers, first one then two inside of her. His mouth pushed her onward while his fingers danced in and out of her body. His strokes became stronger and his fingers traveled deeper until she knew she couldn't take a moment longer. The ache inside her became a fierce convulsion that exploded in an orgasm.

As her breathing slowed, Bianca kept her head resting on his shoulder, not ready yet to look up at him. She felt too humiliated to speak. How could she have allowed him to do something like that to her?

"That was a mistake," she finally said.

"No, it wasn't." He kissed the top of her head then released a ragged breath and touched his forehead to hers.

"Tomorrow I'm picking you up at your office at noon."

She sat up straight and looked him in the eyes. "Why?"

"We're getting married, right?"

Reluctantly, she nodded.

"Then we need to go and shop for a ring."

Chapter 13

The following day Bianca called her office to say that she wouldn't be coming in. First, she had the locks changed. Second, the morning sickness was getting the better of her and she spent the entire day and well into the afternoon puking in the toilet. By lunch she moved out to the couch and lounged across the pillows. Her cell phone rang and she looked down at the ID and saw that it was the man she had agreed to marry.

London Brown.

She gave a loud, strangled groan. How was she ever going to be able to face him again after letting him touch her the way she had last night? Her body still tingled just thinking about the rhythm of his tongue. Heat raced through her as she remembered his fingers buried deep inside her.

She closed her eyes at the memory of his mouth and hand, and she found herself wondering what it would feel like to have something else moving inside her. Never had a man's kisses affected her so strongly. Could she blame it on her hormones and being pregnant? Or was it something else?

Bianca shook her head, as if to shake off the thought. There was no way she could marry him. It was too ridiculous for words. All afternoon her phone had been ringing off the hook and she ignored all the calls from London and her mother. When she listened to the messages she was floored to learn that her mother had arranged to run an announcement of her engagement in Sunday's paper.

Opening her eyes, Bianca stared out the window at the rain beating against the glass. Today would have been a wonderful day to have stayed under the covers and slept, but she just had too much on her mind. So many changes were about to happen in her life, and marrying London was not one she was ready to deal with. She knew he was going to be furious when he dropped by the office to take her ring shopping and she wasn't there. She just couldn't do it. There had to be another way out of this mess she had gotten herself in, other than marriage.

Bianca spent the rest of the afternoon watching silly soap operas and feeling nauseated. It was after five when she finally heard a knock at her door. Bianca glanced through the peephole and expelled a long breath. It was London.

She tried to stop her rapidly beating heart as she took a moment to stare at him without him catching her. All she wanted to see were those lips, and she found herself remembering the kiss they had shared the previous evening. The kiss that left her lying awake most of the night. The same kiss that had been on her mind all day today. He was dressed in khaki Dockers and a crisp white dress shirt and chocolate tie. He looked confident and professional. Yet at the same time he also looked incredibly sexy. She expelled a long breath. Looking through the peephole, she was beginning to think that she was just starting to truly see this gorgeous man for the first time.

"Bianca, I hear you breathing. Please open the door."

She counted to five then took a deep breath, told herself to get it together and opened the door.

"London?" she said and raised an arched brow, as if she didn't know why he was here.

"How are you feeling?" he asked.

She looked up into his intense brown eyes and saw that he was genuinely concerned.

She shrugged her shoulders and stepped aside so he could

enter, then closed the door behind him. "Better now. I only puked half the day." She replied, leading him to her living room.

"Your assistant told me you weren't feeling well. I wish you had called me."

"Why?"

He lowered his head and pressed a kiss to her lips. "Because I'm *your* fiancé and I should not be the last to know that *my* fiancée who's carrying *our* child, is home alone, sick."

She walked over to the couch. His emphasis on *our* made her light-headed. London was claiming her unborn child as his! It caused a warm feeling to flow through her. She didn't like the way her heart was reacting to his statement one bit.

"It's a fake engagement. Our marriage isn't going to be real. And this baby is not yours." She saw the hurt look on his face, and she instantly wished she could take those words back.

"Thanks for putting things back in perspective. I thought you wanted my help."

He was doing her a favor and she was acting like an ungrateful brat just because she was vulnerable and afraid of the things he made her feel. "London, I'm sorry. That was completely uncalled for. I'm just having a bad day and needed to take it out on someone."

He took a seat on the sofa across from her and gave her a goofy smile. "Glad I could be of service."

His comment was met by silence.

"Do you need me to fix you something to eat?"

Her eyes widened. "You can cook?"

He met her curious gaze with a wide smile. "I'm the son of the 'chicken king.' Of course I can cook. My father taught me how to fry fish when I was five."

Bianca playfully rolled her eyes heavenward. "I should have known. Hmm, I've never had a man in my life who could cook."

"Now you do." He rose from his seat and came to stand in front of her. "What can I get you?" he asked, then reached up and loosened his tie.

She noticed the way the shirt emphasized his wide shoulders and swallowed the knot in her throat. "I had soup and crackers a couple of hours ago. I don't think I can handle anything else right now."

"You need to keep up your strength."

His concern for her and her baby's welfare touched Bianca. "I know. But help yourself."

"I wouldn't mind some water if you have some."

She nodded. "There's bottled water in the refrigerator."

While he walked into the other room, she took a deep breath and tried to calm the sensation traveling through her body. Only when she took a deep breath, the spicy aroma of his cologne filled her nostrils.

London returned and took his seat again. She watched while he took two thirsty drinks and finished the bottle. When he met her gaze again, his eyes were intense and her breath caught at the look she saw.

"Why are you looking at me like that?" she asked.

"Like what?"

"Like that."

A smile flirted around his lips. "Maybe I like what I see."

She struggled not to roll her eyes. "I know I look like crap today."

"Bianca, you could be wearing a burlap sack and you would never look like crap."

She smiled. His compliment was sweet.

London looked at her as if he were starving and she were a doughnut in a Krispy Kreme window. A part of her wanted to believe that what he said was true just as badly as she wished the proposal and their engagement were real.

He rose, moved over on the couch beside her and took her hand in his. She gasped. His touch elicited sensations throughout her body and feelings she didn't want to have for him. "We still need to go and shop for an engagement ring for you. I could do it myself, but I want you to get what you want," he said, holding her gaze.

She swallowed and snatched her hand back. "Look, London. This is a mistake. I don't know why I even considered the possibility. But it's stupid and impulsive. No one will ever believe we're in love."

"I beg to differ. I think we'd be quite convincing," he said as he raised a hand and stroked the side of her face.

Her skin heated on contact. "No, we wouldn't."

London met her gaze. "Are you saying you're not attracted to me?"

"I—I didn't say that." She stumbled over her words. She hated being unsure of herself. Every since he'd returned home, London had had women running after him, hoping to snatch the son of the "chicken king." She refused to be anything like those silly, giggling women.

"I'm waiting."

He was so cocky. She wanted to act like it bothered her, but instead it was one of the qualities she found most attractive about him. He'd always been demanding, and right now he demanded to know how she felt about him. She wasn't about to swell his head. He was handsome—that was a given. She was even attracted to him, but neither of those were reasons for them to get married.

Bianca tossed an angry hand in the air. "Stop trying to get in my head! Regardless of whether or not I am attracted to you, that isn't a reason to get married."

"What about the baby?"

Needing to put some distance between them, Bianca rose, strode into the kitchen, and retrieved a bottle of water for herself. She should have known that London was going to follow her. As soon as she shut the refrigerator there he was, standing between her and the door.

He took his time, drawing his gaze from her feet back up to her face and when he finally did, her heart thumped heavily beneath her breasts.

"I often imagine how it would feel to have your legs wrapped around my waist. Or better yet, spread on my bed with them wide open, begging for my lips against your tender flesh."

She was stunned into silence.

"Quit looking at me that way, otherwise I might be tempted to satisfy that hungry look in your eyes."

She gave a strangled laugh. "I'm not looking hungry. And if I am, it's because I need more than soup and crackers."

"Liar! The look you gave me has nothing to do with food."

"That's not true!" she exclaimed. "If I wanted you, I wouldn't beat around the bush about it."

"I think we're good together."

She took another drink and shook her head. "It will never work."

His eyes blazed into hers. "I think it will."

She finished drinking her water and didn't bother to comment.

"Okay, how about this. If I kiss you and you feel nothing, then I will walk away."

"What?" She knew that wasn't about to happen because she still couldn't forget the kiss he'd given her last night. "London, go home. We can try to come up with a different solution tomorrow." She quickly scooted around him and headed toward her bedroom. Feeling self-conscious, she desperately needed to run a comb through her hair. Instead of leaving as she had ordered, London followed her.

"I thought I asked you to leave."

"It's too late for that. We're already engaged."

"Well, I want to be unengaged." There was no way she could be married to him. Not with the way she felt about him. He moved closer. She tried to put some distance between them, but his body was positioned in such a way that she was trapped between him and a wall.

"I don't think that's really what you want." He pulled her into his arms and before she could take her next breath, his mouth came down on hers. On contact, she released a sigh of surrender. Immediately, she softened against him. She closed her eyes and when he touched the tip of his tongue to hers she forgot that he was simply trying to prove a point. All she wanted was to taste him.

He thrust his tongue between her lips and explored the inside of her mouth with intensity. The taste of spearmint flooded her senses. Arching against him, she groaned when his erection prodded her inner thigh.

If she had any sense, she'd shove him away and kick him out of her house after telling him the deal was off. But she couldn't think straight. All she could do was feel, and right now every inch of her body wanted him. Every beat of her heart made her more desperate for his touch.

He pushed a spaghetti strap off her shoulders with impatient hands. The cool air touched her skin, hardening her nipples. But she was far from cold—London made her feel scorching hot. The heat of his hands was on her breasts, stroking, squeezing. Fire raced through her veins. His warm lips traced a hot, wet path from her mouth, down along her neck, not stopping until his lips closed over a taut nipple. Bianca cried out, her head slumping back in pleasure. This was the way it was supposed to be. London laved her nipple with his tongue, gently sucking and nibbling with his teeth, then repeated the torturous play with the other breast. His hands and lips worked her flesh with skill and know-how.

Her legs may as well have been made of gelatin because they were barely holding her up. Only London's grip on her waist kept her from falling onto the floor.

"London?"

He raised his head and Bianca saw desire shining in his eyes. Suddenly nervous, she tried to draw his mouth to hers but he held back, his eyes smoldering with scarcely controlled restraint.

"Do you want me to stop?"

The look in his eyes told her he wanted her. Maybe almost as much as she wanted him. Knowing that made everything in her hum with desire of her own. "Tell me now if you want me to stop," he demanded.

"No, don't stop," she said softly then lifted her hands to his chest. Wanting to feel his bare chest against her, she undid the button of his shirt and pulled it free of his pants then slid it over his wide shoulders and onto the floor. His skin lay bare beneath her touch. She ran her hands over the hard chest and along his flat, rigid stomach. Looking up she met the intensity burning in his eyes and the yearning that had been mounting for the past couple of days exploded inside her. Bianca pulled him down to meet her mouth. He palmed her buttocks as he lifted her and nudged his erection deeper between her thighs.

London drew in a long, deep breath. With a low growl, he moved her until she felt her back against the wall, then reached between them and loosened the string of her sweatpants and pushed them down over her hips. Frantically, she kicked them away and she cried out when London ripped her panties from her body. The fierceness of his actions should have frightened her; instead, it fueled her hunger. Her body arched forward.

He held her with one hand, while he unfastened his buckle and allowed his pants to fall to the floor. Instantly, he kicked them away.

Bianca stood back, licking her lips as she watched him slip out of his boxers. Her mouth dropped and her body tingled at the size of his hard, thick length. Oh, but the rumors were true. London Brown was truly blessed.

With her back against the wall, London grabbed her buttocks, lifting her off the ground. "Baby, wrap your legs around my waist."

Obediently, Bianca locked her legs together around his hips and as soon as she did, he grasped her buttocks with both hands, and entered her in one powerful thrust, filling her completely and pushing her over the edge of reason. She arched her back and hissed in a breath.

"Move with me," he ordered desperately.

He didn't have to ask. Her hips had a mind of their own and were following his rhythm, rocking with him, wanting him deeper.

"Oh, baby," he moaned and tightened the hold on her thighs. The frustrated look on his face, said he was fighting for control.

"What's wrong?"

His eyelids flew open and again she witnessed the desire burning within them. "You. That's what."

She knew exactly what he was feeling because she felt it, too. Yet it was too late to slow down. Way too late to stop at this point. Her eyelids fluttered closed again as she twisted her body and rocked her hips, meeting each pulsating stroke. Cursing, London pulled out and plunged into her again. Her eyes flew open in astonishment as she climaxed, the contractions tearing through her body.

"London!" she cried out, her nails digging into his shoulders. He answered by silently driving into her again and again until she thought she would die from the prolonged pleasure. With one final thrust he came. Clinging to him, she felt the explosive spurt of his orgasm.

London leaned against her, his panting slowly returning to normal. She unhooked her legs from around him, sliding down until she stood and felt a sense of loss as their bodies pulled apart.

Cupping her chin with his palm, he raised her head. Dismay crossed his face at the silent tears running down her cheeks. "Bianca? Baby, did I hurt you?"

"No." She shook her head. "You didn't hurt me."

His thumbs wiped away the moisture on her face. "Then why are you crying?"

"This might sound crazy, but I've never…" Her face burned with embarrassment "I've never…sex has never felt like that before."

Absently, his fingers caressed her cheek and neck. "Never?"

"Never." She struggled to find the words to describe what she had experienced. "It was incredible."

"Really?" He teased her with a smile.

"You're getting a kick out of this, aren't you?" Bianca accused, too happy to take any real offense.

He shook his head, his face suddenly serious. "No, Bianca. I feel honored that I was the first one to give you that pleasure. We've got a lot to look forward to."

Leave it to him to remind her of the engagement and ruin the moment. "I think we need to rethink this marriage thing." After what he'd just done to her, there was no way she could be married to him and leave in a year with her heart intact. She pushed him away, then reached for her clothes and quickly slipped them back on. *What in the world had she been thinking?* But that was it. She hadn't been thinking. It was as if London had cast some kind of spell on her. Panic filled her lungs. She took a shaky breath.

There was no way in the world she would be able to go through with the engagement. Not after what just happened. Not with the things London made her feel. There were so many emotions racing through her that she didn't know how to begin to sort them out, and wasn't sure she wanted to. "I think I'm going to just tell my parents the truth and deal with the consequences."

He hesitated for a long moment. "Are you sure that's what you want to do? I've already offered my services, and I'm a man of my word."

He was definitely that and a lot of other things. She was just starting to see how much more there was to this man. The rumors about his prowess in bed were true. Unwanted jealousy began to surface. She pushed that feeling away.

"Listen, we need…" Bianca's voice trailed off as she heard a door open then close. The next thing she heard was someone walking down the hall calling her name. She turned to London with a look of panic. Quickly, she combed her fingers through her hair and moved to stand in front of the door, just as it was pushed open by her brother.

"Sorry for barging in, but the front door was unlocked and when you didn't answer you scared the crap out of me," Jaden said with a frown.

"What do you need?" Bianca stepped forward, blocking Jaden's path, hoping to block his view of London in her bedroom, as well.

"I wanted to talk about dinner the other night. I was wrong, Bianca, butting into your life and asking London to snoop around." His voice sounded like he was sincere, and most other times she would have been willing to listen to him sweat, but this wasn't one of those times. "Maybe I'm overprotective and need to let you grow up but you're—" The words died on his lips when movement over her shoulder caught his eye. "Is someone in your room?"

"Nope," she said too quickly.

"I think there is." Before she could stop him, Jaden stepped completely inside the room and spotted London just as he was tucking his shirt in his pants.

"What the hell is going on here?" Jaden demanded as his eyes traveled from one to the other until it stopped at Bianca, when he realized her shirt was on backwards. Anger blazed from his eyes. "Why you—"

Before Bianca could step between them, Jaden lunged at London, fists flying. London ducked but not fast enough to avoid Jaden's fist. The blow knocked him backward. He quickly regained control, but she could tell that he didn't want to fight her brother. Instead of balling his fist, he stood up tall, his stance rigid, preparing for another punch.

"Jaden, stop!" she screamed and stepped between them. But fueled by anger, Jaden jumped around her and charged at London again. This time London blocked Jaden's punch with his forearm. "Jaden!" Her screams echoed through the room, but Jaden ignored her and let loose another punch. London ducked, then pushed Jaden away with enough force that he fell back on the bed. Bianca sprang into action and landed on top of her brother, immobilizing him.

"Get off me!" he yelled.

"No, not until you listen!"

He stilled and Bianca stared down at the protectiveness blazing in his eyes. All three of them were breathing heavily. The men glared at each other. Jaden's eyes blazed with suspicion.

"I'm listening. Somebody better start talking."

In a panic, Bianca searched her mind for something, anything she could say because the look in Jaden's eyes told her that as soon as she moved, the fight would be on again, and this time he meant business. "We're getting married," she blurted out.

She heard Jaden's quick intake of breath.

"What? You're kidding, right?"

"No, I'm not kidding. Call, ask Mother, she'll tell you it's true." Bianca rose from the bed and moved over to where London was standing and put her arm around his waist.

Jaden sat up straight on the bed and looked more confused than she'd ever seen him look before. "You and London are getting married?" he asked incredulously.

"That's what I just said."

He looked at her, then at London, then at her again, and started shaking his head and laughing at the same time. "Quit pulling my leg."

"Why? Because you don't think I love your sister?" London said and placed a possessive arm around Bianca and pulled her close.

The laughter died from Jaden's eyes as he stared at London with his arms wrapped around his baby sister. "You're in love?" he looked as if he didn't believe them.

"Yes, we are," Bianca played along, hoping Jaden wouldn't see through her deception.

Jaden leaned forward with his elbows resting on his knees, locks hanging loose around his shoulder. He nodded, but still didn't look convinced. "And when did this happen?" he asked, his tone suspicious.

"Just recently," she answered.

His expression was perplexed, which meant Jaden was thinking. "This is your mystery man?"

"Yes, London is my fiancé," she stated.

He continued to study London. "So you love my baby sister?"

he asked, his tone harsh with disbelief. "Are you planning to marry Bianca?" he demanded.

London returned an unwavering stare, then turned his head and stared down at her. The fire blazing in his brown eyes almost made her gasp. They burned with something she didn't even want to consider as she waited for him to speak.

"Yes, I plan to spend the rest of my life with Bianca."

Bianca shivered. It wasn't what he said but the way he looked at her when he said it.

"I love her," he told Jaden, giving Bianca a look of such sexually explicit hunger that her eyes widened and darkened before she could stop herself from reacting to it.

Jaden rose to his full six-foot-three height, looked at the two of them, hugging as if they were really in love and started shaking his head again. "This is crazy but, hey, who am I to stand in the way of true love," he said, still frowning. "All I got to say is that you'd better treat my sister with respect."

London gazed down at Bianca again and her heart pounded against her chest as she waited for him to respond.

"Don't worry, man. I plan to love her with all my heart." The longer she stared up at the molting passion in his eyes, the more her insides quivered.

She moved away from his sensational heat and turned to her brother. "Okay, now you can get out of my house. And next time, knock," she said, louder than she'd intended to.

Jaden's demeanor softened. "Look, man, I apologize for hitting you. I guess I should've waited for an explanation, but you know how it is. She's my sister."

"Yeah, I know," London replied as the two shook hands, then patted each other on the back.

Jaden reached over and put his sister in a playful head lock. "Damn, Bianca. I had no idea you had feelings for my boy."

"Like I would have told you."

"Yeah, I guess I didn't make things easy for you," he said as he released her. "Look, I'm happy for you—really. That is, as long as you're happy," he commented, eyeing her speculatively. Then his mouth quirked up at one corner. "This is crazy!"

She managed an awkward smile as her gaze found

London's. "Yes, well, we were quite surprised by our feelings for each other."

"How long has this been going on?" Jaden asked, his gaze questioning. It was obvious that he was still trying to get used to the idea.

"A couple of months."

"For a while."

Speaking in unison, Bianca and London looked at each other, their eyes locked in a duel. She swallowed a gulp of air, then turned her attention back to him. Jaden's brow rose and he looked unconvinced. London must have noticed, because he took a step forward, standing by her side. He pulled her against him and lowered his mouth to hers. The intensity of his warm kiss had her swaying when he finally released her.

London shifted his gaze to Jaden. "Jaden, we've known long enough to know that we don't want to spend another moment apart. I can't wait for the day I can make Bianca my wife."

Now he was laying it on thick, Bianca thought. Even the passion burning from his eyes looked real, but she had sense enough to know that it was all an act. Bianca decided it was time to put a stop to it while they were ahead.

"Okay, enough! Can you please get out of here so that we can be alone."

"Sure. I'm out." Jaden was shaking his head and laughing as he stepped through the door and down the hall. Bianca suddenly remembered something and rushed behind him.

"I guess you're going to go and tell Jace and Jabarie."

He snorted a laugh. "Oh, you better believe it! I'm on my way over to their houses now. I can't believe Mother didn't tell me.

"I'll talk to you later." He gave his sister a grin, then opened the door, but stopped before going through it and turned around. "Bianca, I really am happy for you," he said. Then, without waiting for a response, he walked out the door, closing it behind him.

London came up behind her and brought his hands to her waist. "Well, sweetheart. I guess it's official now." The heat of his hands caused her to jump away from his touch.

"Thanks a lot!" she cried.

He looked confused. "For what?"

"For helping me out in there," she said, and dragged a frustrated hand through her hair. "If you hadn't come over here, none of this would have happened."

London gave a strangled laugh. "Oh, so now it's my fault."

She knew it wasn't, but she had to blame her messed-up situation on someone. "You could at least have told him you were fixing a leaky faucet or something."

"Your brother isn't stupid," he countered. "Jaden is old enough to know if he had walked in a few minutes earlier he would have caught your legs wrapped around my waist."

His words caused a strong pulsing sensation down low, and she had to push the image from her mind. Hands on her hips, she started pacing the length of the living room. *Could this day get any worse?* she wondered.

"Hey, you're the one who told him we were getting married—not me."

"I was trying to save your butt!" she yelled, fuming.

"I think I can take care of my own butt." A muscle in his jaw began to tick. He was getting pissed off. Good, now they were even. Moving toward the window, she noticed him rubbing his chin with the back of his hand.

"Are you okay?" she began and moved in for a closer look. "You're going to have a nasty bruise in the morning." She touched his face gingerly and he flinched on contact.

"I've dealt with far worse."

She looked at him as if in a trance before breaking eye contact and putting distance between them again.

"Look, London. We're just going to have to play along for a couple of weeks and then call it off. We can just tell everyone we had a change of heart."

London swiveled around and gave a forced laugh. "Oh? And how do you figure that?" he scoffed. "As soon as the engagement hits Sunday's paper the entire town will know about us."

She shrugged. "So what? Engagements are broken all the time."

"Not ours. We're getting married. I made your brother a promise and I'm not about to go back on my word."

She went still. "I'm not marrying you."

He gave her along hard look. "Oh, yes, you are."

His tone said it wasn't up for discussion. That the decision had already been made. She tilted her chin, challenging him.

"I don't want to get married to you. I'll admit I was wrong for even suggesting such a thing, but now I've come back to my senses."

"Too late. You should have thought about that before you told not only Jaden but your mother that you were marrying me. Now my family knows and probably half the damn town knows. There's no way we're calling the wedding off now."

She was not ready to give up yet. "But I don't even like you."

"You didn't say that earlier when you were crying out my name," he reminded her, his heated gaze running over her skin, heating her up in its path.

"That was just sex." Her tone was defiant.

"It was good sex, sweetheart. The best sex either of us has had in a long time, and you know it."

Her eyes widened as she absorbed the shock of his words. An unwanted sensation traveled through her. "That was a mistake."

"A mistake?" London's laugh was wry. He knew she was lying. He was experienced enough to know when a woman was faking or not. And the way he made her feel, she definitely had not been faking. "So I forced you?"

"I didn't say that."

His brow rose. "So what are you saying?"

"I'm saying it shouldn't have happened."

"But it did happen," London replied, his gaze locking with hers.

Bianca sighed. "Yes, I can't argue that, but what I can promise is that it will never happen again."

He regarded her silently and she felt like squirming under his intense scrutiny. "So you're saying that if I were to touch you right now you wouldn't respond the same way you did less than an hour ago?"

"I'm saying it's not important because it was a mistake and let's talk about something else." With him staring at her, her voice lost some of its boldness.

"No, I want to finish our discussion."

"What else is there to talk about? This engagement is a pretend engagement."

"Were you pretending earlier?" London demanded. The stern

look on his face said he was annoyed that she was trying to act as if what happened didn't mean anything when it fact just the thought had her body already yearning for round two.

"I—"

"Are you saying you were pretending when you begged me to make love to you?"

"London, please—"

"When you screamed my name, were you pretending then?" he asked, studying her.

She had sense enough not to respond to that question.

"Bianca, quit lying to yourself. You enjoyed it just as much as I did."

"I did not," she declared clasping her hands together to keep them from shaking.

"Prove it."

"What?" she gulped.

London let his gaze slowly slide over her. "Prove that it was all mistake. Show me that you feel absolutely nothing for me," he said with the thrill of a challenge beaming in his eyes. She backed away from him. Her mama ain't raised no fool. There was no way she could allow him to touch her again. If she did, there was no telling what would happen. More than likely a repeat performance. "I will not!"

London pinned her gaze with his. "Come here, Bianca."

"No. I think it's time for you to leave." His jaw twitched as he walked over to her without saying a word. Her heart rate increased with each step. When he was standing right in front of her, he reached out and tipped her chin with his hand and she had no choice but to look into his eyes. "I don't think you really want me to leave, either." She tried to remain calm, but couldn't. She bit her lips as she swayed a little. "Come on, Bianca. I want you to show me how much you don't want me."

He moved closer, crowding her space. Trapped, Bianca felt the couch behind her legs preventing her from moving. London gently stroked the side of her face with the back of his hand. Her eyelids closed as pleasure began to slowly flow through her body, starting at her toes.

"Kiss me," he commanded.

"No," she answered, opening her eyes slowly and looking up at him. She was no longer as determined to prove a point as she was before he came and stood before her. Tension began to build as the air in the room became thick and heavy, making it hard for her to breathe. Bianca found her traitorous body leaning toward London, her nipples hardening beneath her shirt as her breasts swelled.

"Kiss me," he said again.

Though his words were still a command, they came out sounding more like a caress. She opened her mouth to demand that he leave and felt his hot breath skim her lips. And instead she released a sigh. Her mouth yearned for his touch. Her entire body pulsed with longing as the heat of his body penetrated her, luring her closer.

She couldn't help but stare at his mouth and those thick juicy lips surrounded by a perfectly barbered goatee. He was gorgeous, and having a perfect mouth only seemed to add to his perfection.

"Show me," he whispered against her nose. "I'm waiting," he replied as he brought his arm around her waist.

"London," Bianca said and gave one last vain attempt at putting some distance between them. But when his hold tightened, instead of pushing away, she rested her hand against his solid chest and tipped her head so that she had no choice but to see him as she spoke. "This whole thing is crazy." Her words came out in a rush of breath.

"Yes, sweetheart, it is." He said and brushed her mouth against his.

He kissed her lips gently, parting them with his tongue with measured strokes. The sweetness inside was intoxicating. What started as a simple kiss suddenly changed so fast she didn't have time to think about what was happening. Instead, her tongue invaded his mouth and he greeted her. She leaned toward him and gripped his biceps and rose on her toes. After a time her lips felt numb. She suspected that he was trying to go slow, give her time to adjust to him, but her body was desperate for more.

Pulling back, their gazes locked. She saw the need and longing in his brown eyes that sent frantic messages to the rest of her body.

Without taking his eyes off her face, he scooped her high

in his arms and carried her into the bedroom. Still holding her, he sat on the bed and pressed his lips to her hair, her forehead, her cheek. He kissed her closed eyes then sat her down gently on the bed.

Finally, he stood and they both undressed. While he stripped off his boxers, Bianca lay naked gazing in appreciation at his thickness. London lay down beside her and gathered her into his arms. She felt him full and hard against her. Her belly warmed and the heat spread downward, creating an ache so deep she had trouble catching her breath. He lowered his head and tongued her nipples until they tightened.

Bianca muffled a cry. She knew she should protest, but when he traced his fingers down her stomach to the apex between her thighs, her delicate folds swelled and tingled. His manhood reared up to nudge her, hard and powerful, making sure she knew what he wanted—to be buried deep inside her. "London," she breathed before she could stop herself.

"Yes, baby?" he asked so gently, her heart skipped a beat.

"I like when you touch me like that," she said, and could not believe she had said out loud what she was thinking. But she couldn't think straight. Not while his tongue ran deliciously along the small of her back. His hands were everywhere, burning a path down her thighs and nudging them apart.

"Spread your legs," he murmured, his voice thick and vibrating against her heated skin.

"No, London," she said but her body had a mind of its own. She parted her thighs instinctively and her back arched, shamelessly seeking him.

"Yes," he murmured.

Her breath rushed in and out when he brushed his fingertips between her legs and trailed them gently along her swollen folds, teasing and sending little shock waves through her body. And she opened for him with a sigh. "Oh, London," she breathed. "Please."

"My pleasure, Bianca," he murmured, his voice husky with desire. The sound of his voice caused her to arch into his hand wantonly. London slipped one long finger into her honeyed sweetness. She stifled a long moan, furious with herself that she no longer struggled against him.

His breathing grew ragged. "Ah, Bianca…" He nipped her flesh with his teeth and then thrust his finger deeper.

She rocked her hips against him as best she could. She knew she should stop him, but she didn't want to put out the fire raging between her thighs.

"You like my fingers here, don't you?"

"No, I don't." She didn't even know why she bothered denying it.

"Yes, you do." He ran his tongue back to her ear and nipped it lightly. He slid his finger out and then up through her sensitive folds. And when he found the small bud that was the center of her pleasure, she flinched. London sighed with satisfaction. "I knew you'd like this."

When he stroked his thumb along her pebbled bud, teasing it, she cried out his name and her body shuddered with pleasure. "London!" Her voice held a whisper. He was driving her crazy and he knew it.

He drew his finger out then dipped his head between her legs. His mouth was on her, licking deliciously as she dug her fingers into his shoulders, tugging at him as he drank in her taste. "London…nooo." Her words drowned on a sigh and she spread her thighs wider. A low moan escaped from deep in her throat as he ran the tip of his tongue along her swollen lips, teasing and flicking lightly over her clit and then retreating. She moaned and arched her hips shamelessly against him as he tasted and teased.

Her body tightened into a torture of sensation as he thrust his tongue with a steady, quickening rhythm, building the pressure unbearably.

"What are you doing to me?"

"Are you going to come for me, Bianca?" he asked. Then he eased his slick thumb into her private entrances. The full shock sent her into a tidal wave of ecstasy. She arched off the bed as his thumb sank up to its full depth.

And when he sucked gently on the center of her pleasure, she exploded around his fingers. "London!" She cried out before she dissolved into wave of pure heat, her body imprisoned by her sweet flames.

"Do you want me, Bianca?"

"Yes, I desperately want you."

"That's not what I mean and you know it. Will you marry me and allow me to be the father to your unborn child."

"Yes…for now."

"You must understand that even though our marriage has a beginning and an end, I plan to be a real husband and that includes making love to my wife."

She was through talking. She couldn't think. Could barely breathe.

"Say it, Bianca," he demanded, perched on the edge, his hands on her thighs spreading her wide. "Tell me you'll surrender to me," he murmured. "Tell me you'll allow me to be your husband even if our marriage is only temporary."

She rocked against him. "Please, London," she pleaded.

"Please what?" he asked as he lowered his mouth to hers and slid his tongue inside. She sucked him hungrily as she rocked her body against his with the strong need to feel him inside her. Her nipples teased the hairs of his chest.

"Yes, I'll be your wife…temporarily. Now, please. I need to feel you inside me, now!"

He covered her with his body and she didn't even think about what they were doing or the consequences. Instead, she focused on being with him and getting what her body so desperately needed. When he rolled onto his back and drew her over him, she eagerly straddled him. She stared down at him, fascinated by every masculine inch. He was so fine. She bent and captured his mouth. Their lips met and their tongues tangled. What she was feeling was too much for words.

She rose over him and London held onto her waist and guided her over his length. He pushed inside and she took him deep. Her eyes widened. Oh, he felt so good. Staring down at him, she ground her hips until he moaned.

"You like that?" she said feeling bold, her fingers traveling down his chest.

"Yes, now ride me."

Bianca rose up until only the tip was in then lowered slowly again. She rose and he guided her with his hand and pumped his hips upward, meeting her halfway.

He groaned and she sped up the pace, rocking her hips back and forth.

Her body began to turn to liquid and she increased her speed, eager to get what only he could give her.

London slipped his hand between them, found her clit and stroked it as she rocked her body against his.

Oh, I could get so used to this. Which was why she couldn't risk her heart. She couldn't allow herself to be in an emotional relationship—not after Collin—but she would worry about that later. All she cared about now was how London made her feel.

When Bianca cried out his name, she heard London cry only seconds after hers. Then his arms came around and held her tightly against him for the rest of the night.

Chapter 14

Hours later, London gazed down into the face of the beautiful woman lying peacefully on the bed beside him and his heart fluttered. Life definitely couldn't get any better than this.

Sleep wasn't even on his mind. He was afraid that if he did fall asleep he would wake up and find out it was all just a dream.

He spent hours replaying the evening in his head, and had to admit that it was one of the best nights of his life. Not that he had thought it would be anything other than fantastic between them. He smiled at the memories.

There wasn't much they hadn't tried last night. Bianca was a woman full of surprises and quite talented. She had showed him a few things he never would have believed possible. Bianca was passionate and erotic and knew how to take over and be in control. Already his penis was growing hard with the thoughts of what the future held for them together. And the heated nights ahead.

All he knew was that from this point on, Bianca Beaumont would be sharing his bed. The rest of their future was uncertain, but it felt right when he thought of the two of them being together, even if it was only going to be for a short time.

Sex was good, damn good. But there was more to their relationship than sex, and he knew that wasn't the only reason he enjoyed holding her, and kissing her, and feeling her warm skin pressed up against him.

He chuckled softly.

A couple of weeks ago, if someone had said he was going to fall for a petite little pregnant woman, he wouldn't have believed it.

But here he was lying beside Bianca Beaumont and he felt like a king.

She stirred and mumbled something under her breath that he didn't even understand. He reached down and pushed a curl from her forehead. Rolling over onto her other side, she pulled the pillow closer to her face and released a deep sigh.

The covers had shifted, and London gazed down at her lying on her stomach, her butt in full view. His penis throbbed at the sight of her and it took everything he had not to spread her legs, slide in between her thighs and bury himself deep again.

She was going to be the death of him.

He could already see it. He needed to keep their relationship in perspective. She had made it quite clear. They were to be married long enough for her to give birth to the baby and for him to give her child his name. As soon as the timing was right, they would go their separate ways.

Why did the thought of losing her sadden him so? he thought with a frown. *He didn't really want to be married. Nor was he ready to start a family. Or was he?*

He shook the thought away. Now was not the time.

Sliding down low on the bed, he pulled her into his arms, satisfied. For the time being, he had her just where he wanted her. In his arms. In his bed. In his life.

Where did that come from? he wondered.

He had planned to keep her away from his heart but he was starting to think it was too late for that.

Bianca brought the mug to her lips and took a cautious sip. Orange rind tea was about the only thing her stomach seemed to tolerate these days. She took another sip, then reached for a cracker. They were the same kind of no-salt crackers London had gotten for her at the diner earlier in the week. That seemed like ages ago.

Last night had been incredible. London was kind and compassionate and a wonderful lover. Her insides quivered just thinking about how she had come apart in his arms again and again until they both collapsed from exhaustion.

After a night of heated passion, she had awakened to the smell of bacon frying and fresh coffee. They spent the morning talking, laughing and washing dishes together before he carried her back to bed, where he made love to her again. She had awakened to find a note on the pillow.

Thank you for a fabulous evening. I'll pick you up for lunch on Monday. No excuses.
Your fiancé

She stared down at the note, now on the kitchen table. London made plans again for the two of them to shop for an engagement ring. It made it seem so real. She was marrying London Brown. Why did knowing that cause her stomach to flutter? Bianca pushed the feeling aside and took another sip. Usually she spent Saturdays doing housework and shopping with Debra, but all she could do was think about London and the magical time they had shared.

Bianca groaned with frustration. *How was it she had gotten over Collin's betrayal so easily?* It was just two weeks ago that she was wearing his ring and planning a future together. Now he was the last thing on her mind.

She shook her head. London had saved her from making the biggest mistake of her life.

After bringing the mug to her lips again, she took a deep breath. She was starting to think that maybe she was about to make another mistake because for the last eighteen hours she had spent way too much time thinking about her new soon-to-be husband.

She groaned with satisfaction as she remembered how London took his time making sure she was sexually satisfied before finding his own release. Afterward, he held her in his arms and kissed her gently, while rubbing her stomach. She almost cried, feeling extremely grateful that London was willing to marry her and give her baby his name.

She knew that she needed to watch herself before she got caught up. He was just helping her out, doing her a favor. Nothing more. After her last disaster of a relationship, falling in love again was not an option.

Love?

She frowned. *Where in the world did that come from?* London Brown was the last man she'd ever fall in love with. But even as that thought flitted through her mind, her stomach quivered. Every time she closed her eyes, she could see his handsome face and sexy eyes. And taste his luscious lips.

The phone rang, breaking into her racing thoughts. Grateful for the interruption, she rose and reached for the phone on the kitchen wall.

"I thought I was supposed to be your best friend," Debra said by way of a greeting.

"You are," Bianca replied and instantly knew she was angry about something.

"Then why is it I had to come to the beauty shop and get my hair done to find out that my best friend is marrying London Brown?"

Bianca moved over to the table and took her seat. "Sorry. I was planning to tell you. We just told our parents yesterday." Actually, she had told her mother and her mother had told the rest of the world.

"Ohmygoodness, Bianca! I can't believe you decided to go through with it. I am so happy for you. Happy for the both of you."

"Thanks…I think."

"You know I'm dying to know what he did to convince you."

"I did it for my baby." But even as she said it, Bianca knew there was more to it than that. She just wasn't ready yet to admit how much London was coming to mean to her in such a short time.

"Come on, Bianca. You're talking to me, Debra, your home girl. I want to know what made you decide to accept his offer."

"Do you have to ask?" she barked with laughter. "My mother." She pursed her lips then added, "And Jaden."

"Jaden?"

She reclined back in her chair and rested her hand on her lower stomach. "I was all set to change my mind when Jaden walked in on me and London in my room…you know…"

Debra gasped. "Y'all were doing the nasty?"

Bianca giggled, wishing she could see the stunned look on her best friend's face. "Yes, we've been doing the nasty."

Debra started screaming and laughing at the same time. "Oh…my…God! Please do tell. Does he live up to the legend?"

Bianca hesitated and warm wetness flowed to her lower region as she remembered him moving inside her. "He's better than the legend." She sat up straight with a start when she realized that she had purred.

Debra screamed as if she had won the lottery, and Bianca joined in.

"Oh, my. This is better than a soap opera!"

"Yep, and it's all because of Collin." Bianca took the next few minutes to tell her about finding him in her house and his threat that sent her running to London's house.

"What did London have to say about it?"

Bianca cleared her throat. "I didn't tell him. Collin is my problem—not his."

"But if he's marrying you, then it becomes his problem as well. That baby is going to be raised a Brown."

A smile teased her lips at the thought. London was definitely a better choice.

She had thought about it long and hard last night. If she got married, she'd have a better chance of keeping Collin from finding out about her unborn child. Then once the baby was born, she and London could separate, divorce and return to their old lives. Only, she realized, she could never go back, at least not to her old life, because now it would be her and a child. Her life would change.

"The sooner we're married the better, which is why we're planning to get married before Memorial Day."

"I guess considering the circumstances…"

She didn't want to be reminded as to why she was getting married. Goodness, the things she was willing to do for her parents.

"I truly believe the two of you are going to be very happy."

"It's not real, Debra. We're only going to stay married long enough for my baby to be born, then we're getting a divorce."

"A lot can happen in that time."

"That won't happen to me. After Collin and all the jerks before him, marriage and love are the last things I need."

"Girl, you know every woman is town going to be jealous of you. You already know what they're saying about him in bed."

She pressed a palm to her ear and shook her head. "I don't want to hear it because it doesn't matter. What happened between us was strictly a bonus. He's just helping out a friend."

Debra snorted rudely in the phone. "Keep thinking that. I can hear it in your voice that it meant a lot more to you than that. What happened last night was more special than you care to admit."

"Debra, I'm pregnant and vulnerable. Right now is not the time for me to confuse my feelings for London and to start thinking there is more going on between us than there really is."

"So you do have feelings for that man?"

Bianca shook her head. "You are impossible."

"Just think how much fun you'll have trying to figure out what you want."

Just thinking about how good he made her feel made her insides quiver. She would just have to find a way to keep her heart intact.

"Well, for whatever reason, I'm just glad it's London and not Collin. I can't wait to see that creep on the street," Debra said.

"He works all the way in Dover."

"That's only a thirty-minute drive. And Delaware is small enough that some day our paths will cross, and when they do, he'd better look out."

Bianca chuckled at how ridiculous her friend was being, which was one reason she loved her so much. Debra always had her back.

"So when's the big day?"

"Three weeks," she said in a breathless whisper. It was still hard to believe.

"Goodness, girl, you're not giving your mother much time to plan."

"Trust and believe, Jessica Beaumont lives for entertaining. Now that the word is on the street, she is going to make sure everything is perfect."

"You know I'm here to help you in any way I can. Like maybe catering the event."

"Good luck getting past my mother."

"I know how to handle Ms. Jessica." It was true. The two had come up against each other on numerous occasions, and Debra always knew how to stroke her mother's ego when the moment called for it—which were most instances.

"I know. That's why I love you. Now hurry up and get your own man."

Debra erupted with laughter. "Nah, I'm having too much fun living vicariously through you."

Chapter 15

Bianca returned to work on Monday to discover two things—a surprise party given by her assistant, Mary, and a copy of her engagement announcement in the society section of the paper on her desk.

The girls in the office had decorated the conference room while Debra brought all the food, including the best coconut cake Bianca had ever tasted. Almost the entire hotel staff, including her sister-in-law, Sheyna, stopped by to congratulate her.

Bianca was touched, by Mary and Debra's thoughtfulness, and her employees for caring enough to celebrate the occasion. If only her marriage were real, then she wouldn't have to feel so guilty accepting everyone's congratulations. For a weird moment she almost found herself wishing that her marriage wasn't a fake.

"Thank you so much," she told Mary. "I can't thank you enough."

They barely had time to clean up the conference room before the public relations department's ten o'clock meeting.

"I'm so glad you've come to your senses," Debra whispered in Bianca's ear as she gave Bianca a big hug, then bid her goodbye. "I'll call you later."

KIMANI
ROMANCE

An Important Message from the Publisher

Dear Reader,

Because you've chosen to read one of our fine novels, I'd like to say "thank you"! And, as a special way to say thank you, I'm offering to send you two more Kimani™ Romance novels and two surprise gifts – absolutely FREE! These books will keep it real with true-to-life African American characters that turn up the heat and sizzle with passion.

Please enjoy the free books and gifts with our compliments...

Linda Gill

Publisher, Kimani Press

EDITOR'S
FREE GIFTS
SEAL
THANK YOU

Peel off Seal and Place Inside...

THE EDITOR'S "THANK YOU" FREE GIFTS INCLUDE:

▶ Two Kimani™ Romance Novels
▶ Two exciting surprise gifts

YES! I have placed my

Editor's "thank you" Free Gifts seal in the space provided at right. Please send me 2 FREE books, and my 2 FREE Mystery Gifts. I understand that I am under no obligation to purchase anything further, as explained on the back of this card.

PLACE
FREE GIFTS
SEAL
HERE

▶ DETACH AND MAIL CARD TODAY! ▶

168 XDL EVGW   **368 XDL EVJ9**

FIRST NAME

LAST NAME

ADDRESS

APT.#

CITY

STATE / PROV.

ZIP/POSTAL CODE

Thank You!

The Reader Service — Here's How It Works:

By ten everyone had returned to their workstations except for Sheyna, who followed Bianca back to her office and sat in the chair across from her desk. The personnel director's office was only two doors down from Bianca and right across the hall from her husband, Jace.

"How is your stomach doing today?" Sheyna asked in a soft voice.

"Better than yester…" She met her sister-in-law's eyes. "You know, don't you?"

Sheyna gave her an innocent look. "I've seen enough pregnant women in my life to know that glow anywhere. How far along are you?"

"Fourteen weeks." Bianca took a deep breath. "I haven't told my parents yet, so I'd like to keep it a secret for the time being, at least until I let them know."

"Your secret's safe with me."

She believed her. The two had been friends long before Sheyna had fallen in love with her brother.

"I'm glad the two of you decided to marry. Raising a child is hard work and I couldn't imagine doing it alone. Your nephew is so spoiled I don't know what to do with that little boy. Jace just adores him. He rushes to day care every evening to pick him up and we fight over who's going to give Jace Jr. his bath. Have the two of you decided on a date?"

"A date?" Bianca repeated, sounding confused.

"Yes, silly, a date!" When Bianca still didn't respond, Sheyna added in a prompting tone, "For the wedding."

"Oh, yes, well, we're thinking maybe at the end of the month."

Sheyna looked pleased by her response. "I would love to go with you to shop for a wedding dress."

"How about tomorrow?"

"That sounds like a good idea," Sheyna replied, eyes dancing with excitement.

There was no way Bianca was wearing the same dress she had intended to wear for her wedding with Collin.

Bianca spent the rest of the morning working on a marketing campaign for the new hotel in Fort Lauderdale. They had hotels all along the East Coast and L.A. and Las Vegas. The plan was to expand to the Midwest in the next two years. Bianca was determined to make that happen. Marketing meant everything to her. The Beaumont Hotel was her life. Showcasing something she believed in was easy.

She was barely six when her father first started bringing her over to the hotel. Like all his children, she started cleaning guestrooms and when she turned fifteen she was working at the front desk. By the time she had graduated from high school, there was nothing that Bianca wanted more than to work for the corporation. She had a vision and knew what it took to put the hotel chain on the map. Beaumont Hotels were now rated among the top twenty best hotels in the country. She would like to think that she was partly responsible for making that happen.

It was close to lunchtime when Bianca put her pen down and stretched her arms above her head. Despite her racing thoughts, she'd had a productive morning. Full-color advertisements were scheduled to run in all the leading travel magazines as well in *Ebony* and *Essence* magazines, in hopes of promoting the Beaumont Hotel as the top African-American hotel chain in the country. Bianca loved working at the corporate office, along with her brothers, Jabarie and Jace. Her father dropped in once a week to see how the corporation was being run. He'd retired officially three years ago and spent most of his time on the golf course.

Reaching inside her small designer purse, Bianca removed a stick of gum and stuck it in her mouth. As she reached for her favorite ballpoint pen, she glanced outside her office door and her hand stilled. London had gotten off the elevator and was heading her way. A tiny feathering of sensation started to uncurl slowly inside her—a potent blend of danger and excitement pumped intoxicatingly throughout her whole body.

Realizing that her mouth was wide open, she pursed her lips as she continued to watch London watch her. She noticed her administrative staff's admiring stares as he strolled past them. Heads turned and followed his every move.

London was fine, and everyone knew it. The gray slacks he wore fit him well and the charcoal, button-down polo hung comfortably from his broad shoulders. By the time he made it to her door, Bianca released a long breath and discovered that she had been holding it.

"Hey, sexy."

She couldn't help but smile. Her eyes were still glued to his. "Hello, London."

He pushed away from the doorway and stuck his hands in his pockets. "You remember why I'm here?"

She nodded. "To buy me a ring."

"Good. I was hoping you hadn't forgotten."

Shyly, she lowered her eyelids. "How could I forget?"

He looked pleased by her answer. "I'm here to take you to lunch, as well."

Nodding, she reached inside her drawer and pulled out her purse. Rising, she swung it over her arm. "Okay, I'm ready."

"No, you're not ready just yet." He strolled over to where she was standing and brought his hands to her shoulders, bent his head and lowered his mouth to hers.

As soon as their lips touched, Bianca was swamped by a tidal wave of emotions. She parted her lips to give him better access. Her entire body was shuddering helplessly as his hands slid from her shoulders to her thickening waist to hold her closely and meld her to his powerful body.

Her fingers reveled in the feel of his muscles beneath the fabric of his shirt and she moaned when she felt his hot, hard arousal against her belly.

She heard London groan just before he lifted his head and stared down at her. Struggling to regain her composure, Bianca was held by the depths of those shimmering dark eyes.

"I missed you," he said and drew in a deep ragged breath.

"Me, too," she heard herself admit only seconds before London took her hand and led her on unsteady legs out the door.

They left the jewelry store and London steered her outside and onto the sidewalk. The street was relatively crowded. Tourists were moving up and down Main Street in cars and on foot, a sure sign that the summer season was right around the corner. Holding hands they strolled up one block and entered Clarence's Infamous Chicken & Fish House and took a seat near the back of the midsize dining room. Red-and-white checkered cloths covered the wooden tables. Memorabilia of rhythm-and-blues players like Louis Armstrong and BB King adorned the walls.

She'd asked for a simple engagement ring, but as she looked down at the beautiful piece of jewelry London had eased onto her finger, she was still in awe. Three emerald-cut diamonds winked in the sunlight. It was the kind of ring that she would have wanted from the man she decided to share the rest of her life with. For a fake marriage it seemed so wrong and the thought of all the people they were going to deceive caused her stomach to churn.

"What's running through your mind?"

"London…" she began, trying to find the right words. "I really think this ring is too much."

His brow narrowed. "Bianca, I can afford it."

Bianca frantically shook his head. The last thing she wanted was for him to think this was about money. "No-no-no. That's not what I meant. I mean this ring is too fancy for a…a marriage of convenience. I don't feel right wearing this ring."

London reached over and cupped her hand with his. "Sweetheart. Fake or otherwise, that is the type of ring a beautiful woman like you deserves. You shouldn't have to settle for anything less."

"But—"

He pressed a finger to her lips. "No buts. You're my fiancée and I want only the best for my future wife."

His words and the passion shimmering in his eyes sent heat thrumming through every cell of her body. "Okay," she said in a low murmur.

He smiled. "Good. Now let's order."

Their waitress came and took their orders and promptly brought their meals. They had been there almost a half hour when Bianca noticed London studying her. "You should eat," he pointed out.

Bianca stared down at her meal, barbecue chicken and potato salad usually tasted mouth-wateringly good, but today…

"Is something wrong with the food?" he asked her, his eyes narrowing.

"Oh, no. It's quite delicious," she began. "It's just that now that it's on my plate in front of me, I don't have much of an appetite."

"Is it your stomach?"

She nodded. "I feel nauseous."

"I'll have Josie bring you something else."

"No-no, please don't make a big deal over it. I can just nibble on some crackers."

Truly concerned for her well-being, he pushed further. "Bianca, you can't live on crackers for the next six months. You're eating for two now. Which means you've got to take care of yourself and the baby."

She heaved a sigh. There was no point in arguing; besides, he was right. No matter how bad she felt, she had her baby to think about. "I'll try a bowl of chicken soup. "

His smiled and signaled for the waitress. "Good answer."

Five minutes later, Josie delivered a bowl of piping-hot homemade soup. It smelled so good, she reached for her spoon and brought it right to her mouth.

"Mmm, delicious."

He looked pleased. "I'm glad you like it. That recipe belonged to my mother's mother."

"It's wonderful," she said between sips.

"I try to use recipes from both sides of my family. I believe that's what a family restaurant is all about. Every few months I introduce something else. My mother has a cookbook that was passed down for generations. I won't run out of ideas for a long time."

She gave him a puzzled look. "I thought this restaurant was started by your grandfather on your father's side."

As he reached for his lemonade, he nodded. "It was, but once I took over I decided the restaurant needed a change and added recipes from my maternal side of the family, as well."

Bianca glanced around at the restaurant, which was filled with customers—rare during the off season. "Obviously, whatever you're doing is working."

He rewarded her with a generous smile. "Thank you. My father told me the same thing when I first broke the news that I was opening a new store. He looked over the books and was amazed at the tremendous growth of the restaurant."

"He should be proud, and so should you. How's the second restaurant coming along?"

His light brown eyes gleamed with excitement. "Fantastic. The contractors should be done by the end of the month. I have to drill at Dover Air Force Base this weekend so I'll just drive up for a couple of days. The rest of this week I'll spend interviewing candidates. As soon as I get a good manager in place, I won't have to spend so much time up in New Castle getting things lined up."

"I can't wait to see it," Bianca said, and she meant it. Something that was important to London was important to her, as well. She wanted to share in his excitement.

"I'm planning a grand opening, but now that we're getting married we need to coordinate the two dates."

Her pulse raced at the reminder of their upcoming wedding. "I was thinking maybe the weekend before Memorial Day weekend?" That was three weeks away.

"Then I'll plan the grand opening for the weekend after Memorial Day."

Bianca nodded. "That's a wonderful idea." She finished up the last of her soup.

"Feeling better now?"

Bianca leaned back in her chair with her hands on her stomach and looked up to find London watching her. "Much better now, thank you."

While he finished the last of his fried chicken and baked macaroni and cheese, she rested her elbows on the table and watched him eat. London caught her staring.

"What's wrong?"

"Nothing. I'm just watching how you and all the people in this restaurant love your family's cooking." She leaned forward before continuing. "I would like to do some marketing for your restaurant."

His brow rose with interest. "Really?"

"Yes. A little marketing can make all the difference in the success of a business. The state of Delaware is exactly ninety miles long. I want to make sure that everyone in either direction knows about Clarence's Infamous Chicken & Fish House."

"I'm listening," he replied and wiped his mouth with a napkin.

"I want to put print ads in all the travel brochures for Delaware and the surrounding tristate area. Also you need to consider coupons in Wednesday's paper. People love thinking they're getting something for free. Like buy one chicken dinner, get one free. Think about it. They'll still want to buy a drink and dessert, only they'll have to buy two now, instead of one. And for your grand opening, let's have a deejay to play some old-school music. That's sure to bring folks out to eat and to snap their fingers. How about a free drink with every meal? And we can also—" Bianca broke off when she realized that London had stopped eating and was staring at her with such an intensity that it caused her insides to quiver. "What's wrong?"

He shook his head. "Nothing's wrong. I'm just admiring how beautiful my fiancée looks when she's passionate about something. You definitely know your stuff."

Smiling, she briefly lowered her eyelids. "Thank you."

"I love all your ideas, especially the part about offering coupons." He brought a forkful of macaroni to his mouth. "Do you think you'll have time with all the wedding planning to do them?"

"For you, I'll make time." It would also give her something to do to take her mind off thinking about him all the time.

"I really appreciate it."

"Hey, what are fiancées for?"

He gave her a dark, bold look. "I can give you quite a few ideas. Meet me at my house after you get off and I'll show you."

The look in his eyes said he had every intention of making love to her. After two days without him, Bianca couldn't think of any reason to say no, except that her heart was in jeopardy. But right now she wanted something so desperately, something that only London could give her.

"It's a deal," she said.

After lunch, London returned her safely to the front door of the hotel.

"See you later," he said, then leaned over and gave her a kiss that was so heated that Bianca was still fanning herself on the ride up in the elevator. When she stepped through her office, Jabarie was waiting inside.

"Hello, big brother," Bianca greeted in a merry tone, as she moved across the plush taupe-colored carpet and around her desk.

"Good afternoon." He rose and walked over to the door and shut the door.

Her brow rose. She never closed her office door unless she was in a meeting. "Is something wrong?"

Jabarie got right to the point. "Are you pregnant?"

She lowered herself into her seat, then put her arms on the desk and nodded. "Yes."

Jabarie ran a hand across his tapered curls and she could tell by the way his jaw twitched that he was trying to keep his anger at bay. "At least he's doing the right thing and marrying you."

She was tempted to tell him who the real father was, but thought better of it. The fewer people who knew the truth, the better.

He paced a path across the length of her office in a black, tailor-made suit. His shoes were so expensive they didn't make a sound. He was making her dizzy. Finally, he dropped down in the chair across from her. "Do you love him?" He surveyed her face.

She hesitated a moment. "Yes. I wouldn't marry him if I didn't."

"Thank goodness. The sooner you're married the better."

Her pride was triggered by the demand in his voice. How dare he tell her what to do? "Of course, we wouldn't want to tarnish the family's name," she said sarcastically.

"You know that's not what I meant."

"What *do* you mean, big brother?"

"I mean I don't want to see you trying to raise a baby by yourself. I want to see you happy."

Her brother's expression softened. She saw the sincerity in his face. And almost felt bad for snapping at him. "I *am* happy." She hated lying, but it wasn't completely a lie. If she was honest with herself, she'd have to admit that for the last few days London had made her feel as if she were on top of the world. "How did you find out I was pregnant?"

"Jace."

She didn't even have to guess how he'd found out. Sheyna. *So much for keeping a secret.*

His smile widened. "I've got good news."

"What? I'm always up for good news."

"Brenna is having twins."

"Goodness, what are you trying to do, start your own baseball team?" she joked. He and Brenna already had an adorable three-year-old girl, Arianna, and a ten-month-old, Brianna. Jace and Sheyna had eighteen-month-old Jace Jr., and Danica and Jaden were six months' pregnant with their first child. "Congratulations. I'm happy for you."

"Thanks. Mother is really going to start feeling old now. She'll have seven grandchildren in the next year."

Bianca brought a fingertip to her lips. "Don't say the *old* word too loud. Mother just might hear you."

"We definitely can't have that."

Smiling, Bianca moved around the desk and gave her brother a big hug. No matter how much her brothers got on her nerves, she knew that they each had her back. *What would she do without family?* she wondered.

Over Jabarie's shoulder, the engagement ring sparkled and reminded her of another family and a fiancé who would be waiting for her when she got off work. She hoped he'd be waiting in nothing more than his birthday suit. The thought caused a traitorous smile to curl the corner of her mouth.

Chapter 16

The week breezed by as she put marketing plans together for London's family restaurants. Unfortunately, the project kept London on her mind 24/7.

Bianca had seen him twice since Monday and each time they ended up back at his house and in bed. After that, he left for Dover for the weekend to fulfill his one-weekend-a-month military obligation. When he returned Sunday night, she eagerly awaited him with open arms. London stayed Sunday and again Monday night. Each time, he made love to her. He was a compassionate, wonderful lover.

After that she declined his offers, feeling that in order not to cloud her judgment she needed to keep a little distance between them. Instead, they talked on the phone and she found that she enjoyed spending hours on the phone with him. They talked about their lives growing up and he told her hilarious stories about himself and his sisters. She didn't need to see him. Just hearing his voice sent sensuous chills all through her body and reminded her of the heated nights she spent in his arms.

By Friday night she was a ball of nerves. She took one final look in the mirror.

She had spent half the morning trying to decide what to wear and had finally decided on a pink linen skirt and a short-sleeve, cream-colored jacket, with a dark pink shell underneath. Cream pumps were on her feet and a pink-and-white scarf was tied in a knot around her neck.

Her eyes traveled over to the clock on the nightstand. London was coming to pick her up at any moment. They were going to have dinner with her parents. And she was a nervous wreck.

It wasn't her parents that had her insides quivering. It was London. She couldn't wait to see him. These past four days had been the longest of her life.

She'd never wanted to be that vulnerable to a man. Especially not London. He was cocky and pushy and wanted things his way. But there were a lot of things about him she truly liked. His conversation, his compassion and especially the way he…

She swallowed and moved out of her room and down the hall. She had better get her thoughts in order quickly. All she had to do was remember what had happened with Collin to know that the last thing she wanted was to be vulnerable to falling in love again. There was no reason for her to come unglued. The doorbell rang. She counted to five, then opened the door.

"Hey, beautiful. You look nice."

She smiled and stepped back as London entered and closed the door behind him. Clearing her throat, she pretended not to be affected by his presence, then gave up because she was only lying to herself. "Thank you. Let me grab my purse," she said, and turned to walk away, but London gently grabbed her by the arm and stopped her.

"Is that how you greet your fiancé?"

She gave a nervous laugh but when she looked up in his eyes, her laughter stopped. The intensity in his gaze caused her to gasp, just as he swooped in and captured her mouth with his. Every cell in her body sang in uncontrollable response. Bianca wrapped her arms around his middle and released a sigh of pleasure. It had only been four days, but with him holding her in his arms, she realized just how much she missed him. London was starting to become important to her and that thought had her heart beating heavily in her chest. London parted her lips with his tongue and slipped inside, and she met his strokes with her own. The kiss didn't end until they both were out of breath.

"Now that's how you greet your man," he said, struggling to catch his breath. "Grab your purse. Time for me to officially meet your parents." He had met her parents years ago, but this meeting would be nothing like that. This evening she would be introducing London Brown as her fiancé.

This was not a good idea, Bianca realized, hesitating in front of the entrance to the country club.

As though London sensed her reluctance, he stepped forward and took hold of her arm so that she had no choice but to enter the club alongside him.

She glanced over at London and felt proud with him on her arm. He was dressed in a brown linen suit and a collarless cream shirt. She admired how well he fit in with all the other men in the room. He could have been mistaken for one of her parents' friends.

Bianca was aware of the stares the minute she and London stepped through the doors of Delaware's most exclusive country club. Her mother had suggested they meet there in hopes of avoiding nosy townspeople. Bianca was glad to take the fifteen-minute drive to Rehoboth Beach. As they moved across the gleaming marble floor, Bianca wasn't surprised when female patrons looked long and hard at London as he strolled across the dining room, holding her hand. He was definitely eye candy.

"Nervous?" he asked.

Bianca gave him a tight smile. "Very. I'm just glad you're here." Very glad. There was no way she could have met with her parents alone. She hadn't seen her parents in two weeks, since she had announced to her mother after dinner that she was engaged to London. And she felt guilty for breaking family tradition by purposely avoiding them. She had no idea how her father had reacted to the news. With each step she prayed for strength.

To her surprise, Jessica and Roger Beaumont greeted them warmly once the hostess delivered Bianca and London to their table. They had chosen a spot at the very back of the restaurant, as if they'd hoped for privacy. Her father rose the way he always did when a lady approached. A smile touched Bianca's lips as she took in the dark black suit that draped his medium build the way it was intended, compliments of a fabulous tailor in town. From the look of her father's salt-and-pepper hair, he hadn't missed his weekly appointment with his barber. His naturally wavy hair was cut low and faded on the side. When their eyes met, he returned her smile and her shoulders relaxed. *Maybe this won't be as bad at I feared,* Bianca thought as she grew nearer. After all, she was a daddy's girl. Bianca moved into her father's strong, outstretched arms and returned his giant hug, then kissed her mother on the cheek. London dropped a peck on her mother's cheek before shaking her father's hand.

"Dear, you look lovely tonight," her mother replied. She knew her mother well enough to know that the moment she spotted her daughter walking across the room she had been inspecting her attire to ensure that it met with her approval. Bianca was relieved to hear that it had.

"Thanks, Mother, so do you," Bianca replied. As always, Jessica Beaumont looked as though she'd just walked down a fashion runway. She was beautifully dressed in a mauve suit with diamond accessories. Her mother wore style and grace as if she had invented them herself.

London helped Bianca into the seat across from her mother, then took the one beside her. The waiter came to the table, handed them menus and took their drink orders. Her parents were already sipping white wine. She and London ordered fresh-squeezed lemonade, and their waiter hurried away to fill the order.

"It's about time our daughter told us who she was engaged to," Roger scolded gently. "I've known your father all his life and I know that he is a good and honest man."

"Thank you, sir."

Her father gave him a dismissive wave. "Please, London, call me Roger. After all, we're going to be family."

Her mother took a sip from a long flute. "Imagine my surprise when Bianca told me she was engaged to you! I was so relieved. Shame on Bianca for leading us to believe that she was marrying a man in the air force."

Bianca looked over at London. Their gazes met as she tried to figure out what he was thinking.

"I *am* in the air force," he began with his eyes still glued to her, then he winked and centered his attention on her parents and smiled. "I'm in the National Guard, instead of on active duty. I left Germany two years ago, after my father had his heart attack."

Jessica reached over and patted his hand. "How is your father doing?"

"Ma'am, he's doing quite well, thank you."

Her mother pursed her lips. "I agree with my husband. They'll be none of that Ma'am stuff. Please, call me Jessica."

They made small talk until their food arrived.

They were halfway through the meal when London suddenly put down his fork and stared intensely around the table. "Sir, if I may say so, I would like to apologize."

Roger's brow rose. "Apologize for what?"

"For not asking your permission to marry your daughter."

Bianca choked on a roll.

"Sweetheart, are you okay?" her mother asked.

She nodded and reached for her glass.

"Mrs. and Mrs. Beaumont, I love Bianca and plan to spend the rest of my life showing her just how much," he said.

Bianca was speechless. He turned in his seat and pressed his lips to her cheek and her skin tingled. She stared up at him in awe. The impact of his look caused her mouth to go dry. His eyes were bubbling over with passionate intensity, and something else she couldn't describe. It was as if he truly loved her. And her insides quivered. She couldn't help but wonder what it would be like to have a man who truly loved her. To have a man look at her the way he was staring at her and really mean it. She shook the ridiculous thought away. London didn't love her, she reminded herself, nor did she want him to. This was only a show for her parents.

"Bianca, dear, quit staring at that man before you run him off," her mother scolded, chuckling.

"I agree," her father chimed in. "This is the best one you've brought home yet."

Bianca shook her head and focused her attention on her salad.

The way her stomach was churning she couldn't handle much more than that.

Her father was obviously pleased that London knew how to show respect. Roger rose and offered him his hand. "London, son, we would be more than happy to have you join our family."

Bianca watched as the two shook hands. Even her mother had tears in her eyes. All along she had thought her parents would disapprove of her marrying a man outside their social class. Instead, they genuinely looked pleased.

Who are these people and what have they done with my parents?

Her mother folded her hands in her lap and Bianca could already see the wheels turning in her head. "Well, we definitely need to plan a wedding. How about September, or a winter wedding like the one Jabarie and Brenna had?"

London's gaze confronted Bianca's. She opened her mouth to speak when he reached for her hand underneath the table and laced his fingers with hers. "Mrs. Beaumont, we were thinking more of getting married right away."

She looked from one to the other, frowning. "Why so soon? If you want a nice wedding, I need time to plan."

Bianca took a deep breath.

"Mother, Dad…I'm pregnant."

"Preg—" Jessica's voice trailed off as Bianca's words sank in. Surprise registered on her mother's face a split second before she concealed it and shot her husband a warning look. Despite her attempt to smile, her lips thinned.

"We haven't decided on a date yet," Bianca said quickly, trying to think of something. "Mother, I was hoping you could help with that."

Her father cleared his throat. "I agree. Considering the circumstances, I think the sooner you two get married the better."

In other words, before she started showing.

Her mother's eyes fell to her stomach.

"I'm fifteen weeks' pregnant," Bianca replied to her silent question.

"Then that doesn't leave us much time."

London squeezed her hand and she was thankful for his support. "I would agree," he said.

"Good." Jessica looked pleased by London's answer. "What date do you have in mind?"

Bianca swallowed. "The weekend before Memorial Day."

Her mother mistook the saddened look on her face for something else. "Sweetheart, time is of the essence considering…" She purposely allowed her voice to trail off and at the look on her face she tossed a hand in the air. "Don't worry. I'll make all the arrangements," she announced.

"Nothing fancy," Bianca warned. She knew her mother too well.

"Okay," she said with a sigh of despair. "I'll keep it simple." Leaning back in the chair, she rested her hands on her stomach. "I want to get married at home in the garden."

Her mother smiled, pleased by her request. "That sounds like a wonderful idea."

Bianca glanced over at London for confirmation and he nodded. She was relieved. She had always dreamed of being married in a church, but there was no way she could do that when she knew her marriage was a fake.

Her father reached across the table and patted her hand. "Well, then, it's settled. You and your mother have a wedding to plan."

"Do you mind if we stop at the bookstore?" London asked after they left the country club and made their way to his car. He walked around to the passenger side and opened the car door. "My sister's birthday is this weekend and I know she's been waiting for this new romance novel to come out."

Bianca nodded as she pulled the seat belt across her body and secured it.

London waited until he pulled away from the parking lot, then asked, "How do you think things went in there with your parents?"

"I think you won them over. Mother is easy. Just knowing that I'm getting married and not running around having illegitimate children is enough to ease her mind. All she ever cares about is looking good in front of people and planning the social event of the year."

He frowned. "You're being kind of hard on her."

"Oh, really? Here," she began as she shoved her cell phone in front of his face. "Call my mother and inform her that

Clarence's Infamous Chicken & Fish House is catering the reception dinner."

He looked from the stubborn tilt of her chin down to her phone and back again. "I see your point." He hadn't been gone that long that he didn't remember her mother's need for only the finest things in life.

"I'm surprised she thinks I'm good enough for you."

"I'm pregnant. Of course she's going to accept you." He made a turn at the corner. Bianca stared out the window and gave a simple shrug. "Now, my father is another different story. Five years ago, he would have had you thrown out of the country club and had you up on rape charges. But ever since Jabarie and Brenna got married and gave birth to Arianna, he has done a total 360-degree turn around."

"That's a good thing. Jaden used to mention all the time that his father worked too hard and never spent much time with the four of you."

"That's true. Now he calls so much that sometimes I wonder which is worse," she replied with a chuckle. "Sheyna mentioned that sometimes she and Jace are in the middle of getting it on and here comes Daddy pulling up in the driveway."

London shared a laugh. "I see what you mean." Then he reached over and grabbed her hand. "I guess that while I'm busy making love to my wife I can expect her father to magically appear."

His words caused her to shift on her seat and stare up at him. When London called her *his wife,* it sounded so right, so natural.

Obeying the twenty-five-mile-an-hour speed limit, London pulled onto Main Street. Bianca's eyes traveled along the wide cobblestone street. He pulled up at the bookstore, came around to her side and helped her out.

"Thank you."

"Hey, look at me." He tilted her chin and she raised her eyes and met the serious expression on his face. "It's going to be okay. You'll see." He lowered his mouth to hers, planted a quick kiss on her mouth and released her. Quick or not, she felt the sensation down to her toes.

They moved across the sidewalk and London opened the door and stepped into the quaint little bookstore behind her. They had barely entered the building when Brenna came rushing over to greet them.

"Bianca!" Her big hazel eyes lit up with excitement as they met. "Jabarie told me the news."

"Jabarie told me *your* good news. Twins! I'm so happy for you." Bianca gave her sister-in-law a kiss on the cheek. "Okay, I need your bathroom." She scooted off, leaving her sister-in-law and her fiancé together.

"London, you get over here right now and give me a hug!" Her grin was as welcoming as a cool breeze on a sweltering summer night.

Before London had a chance to prepare himself, Brenna had reached over and pulled him to her. When she finally released him, London stepped back and looked down at her smiling face. Her eyes were sparkling with excitement.

"Oh, my goodness! You and Bianca are getting married," she went on, not giving him a chance to speak. "I'm so happy for you both."

London gave her a slight nod and a grin. "Thanks" was all he could manage to say. He and Bianca still had a lot to discuss and he wasn't sure what he should be saying.

"What brings the two of you to my little store?"

"I need to pick up a book for my sister, Mona." London told Brenna what book he was looking for.

"Oh, yeah, she is one of our most popular romance authors. Follow me." He went with her to the romance section.

"Wonderful. You're going to make my sister very happy."

She plucked the book from the shelf and they were moving over to the counter when Brianna, Brenna's ten-month-old daughter came into view. The child had been sitting quietly in a playpen.

The next thing he knew, Brianna was holding her arms up in the air, wanting to be picked up. Automatically, he bent down and picked her up. She placed her hands on his cheeks and kissed him on the lips.

London kissed her back. "Thanks, sunshine."

Bianca came around the corner and smiled when she saw the two of them together. "My niece is already a flirt. Wait until I tell her daddy."

"Don't even go there," Brenna warned as she rang up the purchase. "Jabarie's already staring down every little boy at day care. He laid down the law—no boys at her birthday party."

They laughed. Brianna held out her arms for her aunt, and Bianca took her and kissed the baby on the top of her head. London stared intently at the two of them together.

Bianca looked his way and he swallowed. She had a life growing inside her and he was going to play a major part in that child's life. He couldn't begin to explain the overwhelming feeling that swelled up inside him.

"Look at you two lovebirds staring at each other! Everybody is talking about your news. It is going to be the event of the year. I am so excited," Brenna remarked, taking her daughter and kissing her cheek. Their resemblance was uncanny. They had the same hazel eyes, light brown hair and small nose. Brianna was going to be a heartbreaker, London thought.

"Thanks," he muttered, as he studied Brianna's smiling face. As he looked at the baby, he thought about Bianca. She could be carrying a little girl. His heart jumped at the thought.

"To tell you the truth, I thought something was going on between the two of you," Brenna commented, interrupting his thoughts.

London's head whipped around and his eyes connected with hers. "What?" he couldn't possibly have heard right. What would have made Brenna think that?

"Oh, come on, you two," she told him, a teasing smile on her lips. "I've seen the two of you out together before, trying to act like you were just friends when all along something else was going on. Boy, you sure had me fooled at first, but the way I saw the two of you looking at each other at Jace's wedding, I knew there was more to the story."

He met Bianca's raised eyebrows and couldn't pull his eyes away. *Had there really been something more going on back then that he wasn't aware of?* Sure, he had been attracted to her, but maybe in the back of his mind he always knew that beneath the surface he wanted to explore the possibilities of a relationship with her.

London gave a nervous laugh. "I guess our secret's out."

Coming from behind the counter, Brenna draped an arm

across Bianca's shoulders. "Yes, it is, and it couldn't have happened to a better woman."

Their gazes met and held. "I definitely have to agree with you there."

Fifteen minutes later, London pulled in front of Bianca's town house and left the motor running. As much as he wanted to follow her inside to her bed, he decided that maybe that wasn't such a good idea. All kinds of crazy thoughts were racing through his brain. And that was not a good thing. He needed to keep his head on straight and remember that this was a marriage of convenience. One friend helping another friend and nothing more. Well…maybe a little more. Staring down at the swell of her breasts, he licked his lips and found himself wanting to take one in his…

"Hey, Earth to London," Bianca said and snapped her fingers in front of his face, drawing his attention. "I asked if you wanted to come in."

He stared down at her mouth and was tempted. So very tempted. "No, I'd better not. I have to drive down to New Castle tomorrow and check on the restaurant."

Bianca looked disappointed, and he almost told her he'd changed his mind. Instead, London leaned over, pressed his lips to hers and gave her a long, searing kiss. The blood in his veins ignited and fierce desire pulsed through his body. He forced himself to pull away. He was held by the brown of her eyes, surrounded by thick lashes. He could drown in her gaze. He was about to change his mind when Bianca climbed out of the car and headed toward the door.

"Good night, Little Mama," he called after her.

She glanced over her shoulder and grinned, then practically skipped all the way up the steps and into the house. London was already regretting not following her. He was in for a long sleepless night and a cold shower.

Chapter 17

Bianca opened the door and London took one look at her and felt as if he'd received a hard punch to his gut. He dragged in a deep breath. She was both beautiful and sexy, especially in snug-fitting blue jeans, and a yellow tank top. His gaze strayed to them and stayed there a moment too long, long enough to see that she was wearing a strapless bra. Long enough for him to remember what it felt like to suck her nipples into his mouth.

Quickly, he dragged his eyes to her smiling face.

"Is something wrong?"

He shook his head. "No, sweetheart. Everything is just right. But if we don't leave this very second we won't leave for at least another hour."

She stared up at him and her lower lip trembled nervously. Obviously, the hunger blazing in his eyes didn't go unnoticed.

"Then I'd better grab my purse so we can get out of here. You wait out here," she ordered then shut the door.

London gave a frustrated groan and moved back out to his SUV. *What was happening to him?* He always had an active sex drive,

but being around Bianca put his libido in overdrive. All he did was
think about making love to her. He'd never felt like this before.

London moved behind the wheel at that thought. He was
driving himself crazy trying to keep everything in perspective.
But despite how much he tried to deny it, London was starting
to enjoy the new role Bianca was playing in his life.

"Bianca, this is my big sister, Mona Lisa."

Mona rushed forward and hugged Bianca tightly. When she
released her, Bianca studied the woman, finding her beautiful.
She was tall and slender with a toasted-pecan skin tone and bril-
liant light brown eyes. "Welcome to our home, Bianca. My
brother said you were pretty, but I had no idea just how pretty."

"Thank you."

She stepped into the foyer of the three-story home where he
had grown up and Clarence, London's father, came around the
corner. "Well, well, if it isn't Ms. Beaumont." She found herself
swept up into a gigantic hug.

"It's so good to see you, Mr. Brown. How have you been?"
she asked once he released her.

"Fine, just fine."

Gazing over at him, Bianca noticed a sprinkling of silver in
his close-cropped gray hair. He had never been a small man and
since she'd last seen him he had added several inches around his
middle, giving him the look of a cuddly teddy bear.

"You look different from the last time I saw you," he said,
patting her arm. When she blushed, he winked. "All grown up
and lovelier than ever. I might have to steal you for myself." He
laughed, then leaned in and kissed her on the cheek.

"Easy, Dad," London said, coming over and draping a possessive arm around Bianca's waist. "This one is taken." Someone
sitting in the living room laughed.

"That's too bad!" his father joked and gave Bianca a playful
wink. "Don't pay me no mind. I'm just glad to have you here.
It's been a long time since this one brought a woman home."

"Thanks for having me and please call me Bianca," she
said, adoring everything about the kind old man. London's arm
tightened around her and she turned and looked up at him. His

expression was unreadable. She wondered what he was thinking.

"You two can stare at each other later," his father said beaming. "Come on in. Everyone has been waiting for you to arrive."

She could hear voices coming from the living room and took another look at London. He gave her a reassuring smile, then draped his arm lightly across her shoulders and led her into the living room, where a handful of people had gathered and were sharing photo albums. All eyes were on them when they stepped into the room. Everyone started saying hello at the same time.

"This is my sister, Denise," London said, referring to a petite feminine version of himself. "And those funny-looking girls over on the couch there are my big-headed twin sisters, Camille and Carmen."

The beautiful women with smooth, cinnamon complexions were far from funny-looking. The taller one gave Bianca a hug, then narrowed her eyes in the direction of her brother. "Welcome, Bianca. I'm Carmen. If my brother keeps this up, I'm going to be making you a widow before your wedding day."

"That's for sure," Camille added as she gave Bianca a warm hug, as well.

Bianca giggled. Anyone could tell they loved their brother, who probably spent his entire life picking on them. There were both pretty. Identical twins. Round faces, dark, slanted eyes and long dark brown curls. Carmen wore hers in a cute ponytail, while Camille allowed hers to hang loose around her shoulders.

After they exchanged a few words, London led them inside the family room. Bianca was in awe. The room had been decorated with balloons and a large streamer congratulating the happy couple. There was food and a large sheet cake. She didn't have a chance to take it all in when London started introducing her to the clan. There were so many Browns there that one would have thought they were having a family reunion.

There were his four beautiful sisters, his cousins, aunts and uncles and a few close family friends. Bianca had never seen so many people in one room. Everybody was friendly and welcomed her to the family, although Bianca was certain that she would never remember everybody's name. Especially not with

London's arms draped possessively across her shoulders. London was standing so close that she could feel the heat from his body. His musky scent surrounded him and she half feared she would become dizzy.

"It's about time you got here."

London looked toward the kitchen door and frowned. "Mark," London acknowledged when the tall, solidly built man with eyes the color of a copper penny came to join them.

He finally left her side long enough to give the man a hug, and she took that moment to try to calm her hormones. This was not the time or the place for the erotic thoughts she was having.

"Bianca, I'd like you to meet my womanizing cousin."

Mark's gaze went straight to Bianca. "Never that. I'm always honest with my dates," he said smoothly, as a smile touched the corners of his mouth.

"Yeah, right," London replied with a bark of laughter.

"Hey, it's not my fault they don't care to listen."

Bianca chuckled. "Nice to meet you."

He shook her proffered hand "Welcome. What would you like to drink, maybe a wine cooler?"

Bianca didn't know what to say.

London dropped a kiss on the top of her head and must have noticed that she was a bit flustered at all the attention because he pulled her closer. "A lemonade for my future wife and I'll take a cold beer if you have one."

Mona laughed. "We've always got cold beer." She glanced at her cousin before making her way into the kitchen. "Mark, point them in the direction of the food. London, give poor Bianca some air."

Bianca looked up at London. The grin on his face was impossible to read. She swallowed and wondered again what he was thinking. She was smiling, as well and had to admit that it felt good to be around him and his family.

While holding her hand, London introduced Bianca to several other people who were already gathered around the table, filling their plates. The buffet contained an assortment of platters—meatballs, potato salad, barbecue chicken, baked beans and several other dishes. Although the food looked delicious, just seeing it all was enough food to make her feel sick. She reached for the cheese and crackers. London, who had been watching her intensely, leaned over so that his mouth was at Bianca's ear. "You okay?"

She nodded, even though her insides were a ball of nerves and she was weak-kneed from standing so close to him.

"Don't hesitate to let me know if you're not feeling well. I have no problem leaving and taking you home," he said.

Bianca nodded. Again there was something about the way he always cared about her and her unborn child that warmed her heart in ways she couldn't begin to describe. Seeing the softer side of him only confused her even more about her feelings for him. If she wasn't careful, she would fall in love.

Mona appeared with their drinks. "Everything smells and looks delicious," Bianca told her as she took the lemonade from her. "I really appreciate your going to all this trouble."

She waved Bianca's concern aside. "Oh, it was nothing. Everybody pitched in."

As Bianca prepared her plate, she couldn't help but notice how different their two families were. Jessica Beaumont would never have asked her family or friends to bring food to one of her parties. She would have called a catering service or used her kitchen staff. She would never have served beer, either. But this warm gathering of friends and family, who'd spent hours in their kitchens cooking for her and London's engagement party, meant more to her than any meal any five-star restaurant could have prepared.

London stayed by her side, laughing at the jokes his family told. "Don't let them embarrass you," he whispered, his mouth touching her ear. "They're just having fun."

She shivered on contact, his lips on her outer ear, and his breath warm on her cheek. "I know."

She found a spot on a couch in the family room and nibbled on her food. The barbecue ribs were good and tender. Dinner conversations were light and entertaining as she listened to the family jokes about London growing up. She hadn't been able to keep any food down all day, but she managed to finish almost everything on her plate. The Brown family definitely knew how to throw down in the kitchen. When she couldn't eat another bite, Bianca carried her plate to the kitchen, where she found London's sister, Denise, rinsing dishes and putting them into the dishwasher. "Everything was delicious," Bianca said.

"Thank you. I'm glad you enjoyed it," the woman replied, taking the plate from her. "I'll have to be honest. We were all shocked when London told Daddy he was getting married, so all of us were dying to meet you."

"It all happened so quickly," Bianca said.

Denise smiled. "Yes, it did, but after seeing the two of you together, it's obvious that you're crazy about each other."

"It is?" In Bianca's surprise, the words slipped out.

"Well, of course. I didn't even know my brother was seriously dating anyone and the next thing we know, he's engaged. If that ain't love, I don't know what is. I've never seen London this happy."

Bianca's eyes traveled into the other room, where London was laughing at something his cousin Mark had said.

"My sisters and I are so happy for him. At least now Dad might get off our backs for a little bit." When her statement was met by a puzzled look, Denise continued. "We're not married."

Bianca was flabbergasted. "You mean to tell me that none of you are married?"

"Nope. We've been so busy with our careers that a man has been the last thing on our minds. Maybe in a few years, but right now we're all enjoying being single."

Bianca knew what she meant. She had felt the same way until she met Collin. But her feelings for London were even stronger than what she'd felt for Collin. Could she be falling in—

Nope. She refused to even entertain that thought.

"Don't get me wrong. We're all happy. After the cancer took Mama from us, the twins decided to live at home with Daddy, and Mona and I each have places not too far from here. We still eat dinner together at least three times a week."

"It seems like your family is really close."

She nodded. "We are."

London came into the kitchen at that moment. He noted the look on Bianca's face. "Is something wrong, honey?"

She smiled at the endearment. He had been so attentive all evening that it was hard to remember that he was just playing a role.

"I was just thanking Denise for going to all this trouble."

"Don't get carried away," he said. "She and my sisters owe me."

She shot him a dirty look. "You're never going to let me off the hook, are you?" She looked to Bianca. "A couple of years ago London saved the life of a man who was choking. And before you ask, it wasn't in our restaurant. Anyway, the man just happened to own two car dealerships and has given the entire family great deals on new cars ever since. London thinks we owe him for the rest of our lives."

He pointed a finger at her. "You do owe me. I saved you thousands."

She rolled her eyes. "Whatever."

Bianca laughed, enjoying the way they teased each other.

Mark called London into the other room. Bianca offered her assistance and helped Denise clean up the kitchen. While the women talked, Bianca often looked over to where London was standing and her heart thumped an unsteady beat just watching him. As if he felt the heat of her eyes, he cocked his head in her direction and their gazes connected. Goose bumps rippled along her arms and she expelled a long, silent breath before breaking eye contact with him.

Needing to distract herself, as soon as Denise refused any further help, Bianca escaped out onto the balcony. Once there, she swallowed a gulp of fresh air and wondered where in the world her good sense had gone. The wind caught a strand of her hair. She reached up and brushed it away from her face.

Leaning against the wooden railing, she stared out at the view. The Browns' house sat on two acres, and the huge ranch-style home was simply gorgeous. Obviously, the interior, decorated in strong, bold colors, were creative choices made by the four Brown women. The deck provided a lovely view of a lake. She stared at the water. The moon was overhead, shining down on the lake. A cool breeze rattled the trees and she listened as her mind wandered.

If only this were real. She and London really engaged and sharing a celebration with his family. The very thought warmed her heart. Frantically shaking her head, she shook the ridiculous thoughts away and blamed it on her pregnancy.

Bianca knew it was dangerous to be thinking about London

that way, but she just couldn't help it. Not with his family gathered around them, talking about love, family and marriage. Three weeks with him had given her an idea of what it would be like to make love to him and share the rest of his life.

She wasn't the right woman for London and she damn well knew it. Just because they had great sex together, and she couldn't stop thinking about him, didn't mean they were right for each other. Besides, she'd never be able to give him her heart. He deserved a lot more from the woman he'd spend the rest of his life with.

"What are you thinking about?" London whispered near her ear, as he sauntered up quietly behind her.

Bianca's breathing halted momentarily before starting up again. She hadn't heard him approach. The warmth of his breath touched her neck, and she closed her eyes and felt her body naturally sway back and rest against him. "I'm not thinking about anything. Just came out to get some air."

"I don't believe you," he replied, bringing his arms around her and securing them at her waist. He felt so good her skin tingled.

"Then that's your problem that you don't believe me, not mine."

London swung Bianca around and she leaned back against his splayed fingers. He stood in front of her, flashing a wide smile. For a long moment they stared at each other, neither saying anything.

"Are you having second thoughts?" he asked softly.

"Yes and no."

His eyes narrowed with concern. "Care to explain?"

Before she began, Bianca dropped her eyes to his chin where his goatee was trimmed nice and neat. She longed to stroke him there. "I'm just trying to make sure that I'm not making a mistake. Getting married is a big step and I don't want you to regret being shackled to me."

"Hey." He cupped her chin and tilted her head up so she had no choice but to look at him. His eyes darkened until they were nearly black with an indefinable emotion. "Nobody makes me do anything I don't want to do. I offered to help you and nothing has changed. In fact, I'm looking forward to a lot of long, passion-filled nights with you," he said.

Her skin prickled and sizzling nerve endings tingled along her spine with anticipation. She looked forward to the same thing.

"Who wouldn't look forward to that?"

London looked down at her and her female hormones surged with need. Still cupping her face, he took her mouth in his, driving into it with the slow thrust of his tongue. Leaning into him, Bianca moaned with delight at the feel of his lips against hers. She was lost in his kiss. When he finally broke it off, she looked up at his mouth, staring at the moisture on his bottom lip.

"Does that answer your question?"

Mark stepped past the sliding-glass door, onto the deck, breaking the spell. "We need y'all in the living room." He motioned for them to follow.

Recovering quickly, Bianca shot London a questioning look. "I have no idea." He took her hand. "Might as well go find out."

As they walked into the living room, Bianca saw that everyone seemed to be waiting. Clarence stood in the center with his hands folded in front.

"Here are the lovebirds. Come on over here, you two, and have a seat on the couch." He waited until London and Bianca were by his side before he began. "I just wanted to say that we were all thrilled to hear about your engagement. It was a surprise, but we're happy for you and wanted to say congratulations."

Bianca smiled shyly at the group. "Thank you very much," she said. London echoed her sentiments and everyone clapped. Bianca heard the sound of popping corks and saw Mona and the twins pouring champagne into disposable glasses.

"Before we toast, I would like to say a few words," Clarence said, only to be met by groans from his daughters. London chimed in. Bianca had a feeling that her future father-in-law was somewhat long-winded when he wanted to be, and giggled. Clarence ignored them and faced Bianca. His look softened. "Bianca, I want to personally welcome you to our family. We don't have much, but one thing we never are short of around here is love," he added, glancing at Mona who offered him a thoughtful smile. He paused when Mark carried over a tray of champagne glasses and waited for them to each to take one. "We all wish the two of you the best of luck. I know you'll be happy and make plenty of beautiful babies." He looked around as if to see that everyone held a glass. "London, Bianca—" he held his glass high to toast them "—please accept our sincere congratulations on your engagement and may you have many happy years together."

Bianca felt a wave of heat sweep up her chest and settle at her cheeks as the group toasted them. She felt bad deceiving all these good people.

"Thank you," she replied and brought the glass to her lips. They would all wonder why if she refused. She was sure one sip wouldn't hurt the baby.

London rose and tilted his glass to the crowd. "Thanks, everyone. I look forward to spending the rest of my life with this beautiful woman." His voice was soft and layered with sensuality.

London reached for Bianca's hand and she rose from the couch. He then took her glass and his and set them on the coffee table. Bianca was stunned when he slipped his arms around her, pulled her hard against him and kissed her soundly on the lips.

Surprised, Bianca's mouth opened slightly and London slipped his tongue inside, pulling her even closer. She was only vaguely aware of the clapping and wolf whistles as London pulled her even tighter in his arms.

Bianca felt her knees turn to pudding. She almost groaned out loud when she tasted the sweet champagne on his lips. Something inside her snapped, and her body came to life as she felt this overwhelming need to keep on kissing him.

Mona made a show of clearing her throat. "Excuse me, but there are other people in the room besides the two of you," she said reminding them that they were not alone.

"Get a room," someone yelled.

Bianca placed a palm on his chest, pushing against his solid muscle. London raised his head. He and Bianca made eye contact. It was as if she were seeing him for the first time. From the look on his face, she knew he felt it, too.

London noticed that Bianca was relatively quiet on the ride home.

"Did you have a good time?" he asked.

Even though her eyes were closed, she smiled. "Yes, I did. I really like your family."

"And they like you." Before they had left, his father had pulled him aside and told London that he was proud of him and that he had made a good choice.

"I hate deceiving them. They think we're really in love." There was a hint of frustration in her voice.

"I know," he replied with a degree of guilt. It bothered him, as well—deceiving his family. He hadn't seen his father look that happy since…since before his mother died.

As she sat there quietly, with her eyes closed, London thought about their kiss.

Bianca had gotten under his skin. There hadn't been a single night since they first made love that he could think of anything but her. Angrily, he fought against the longing to possess her permanently. That would be a mistake. Theirs was a business arrangement—nothing more.

He was glad when he finally pulled into the driveway.

"Next weekend's the big day," he said in a low voice. Bianca turned her head and he met her clear gaze. For a short time he was lost in the moment. He wanted her like hell on fire. And if he touched her again, he wasn't going to be able to control the impulse to carry her into the house and make mad passionate love to her for the rest of the night. Yet he couldn't sort out the emotions swirling within him. He needed some time to put those emotions in perspective.

Bianca must have seen the lust burning in his eyes because she licked her lower lip nervously before swinging her purse strap over her shoulder. "Yes. I'll be busy working on a project most of the week so if I don't see you before the rehearsal dinner…"

He nodded. "I understand." A little distance was probably for the best. It would give him a chance to get his head together before Bianca became Mrs. London Brown.

Chapter 18

"You look beautiful," Brenna whispered as Bianca stepped out of the bathroom into the sitting where her three sisters-in-law and Debra were waiting.

While they oohed and aahed, Bianca moved over to the floor-length mirror and viewed her best friend's skills at doing her hair. Debra had pulled her hair back and secured it with pearl-beaded pins. The look was classy and cute.

"Wow!" Danica began. "I love your dress."

"Thanks," she said, glancing down at the wedding dress that she had found while out shopping with Sheyna. It had taken her two days before the wedding to find it at a small bridal shop in Ocean City, Maryland. As soon as she spotted it in the window, she knew she had to have it. The beige silk gown was ankle-length with a train, delicately beaded and extremely low in the back. The fabric accented her figure and flared slightly around her ankles. It wasn't anything fancy or breathtaking, but it made her look and feel beautiful. Being four months' pregnant, she needed that.

Bianca turned to the side and captured the side view. Thank

goodness her stomach was still relatively flat. It would have been a disaster if she had been showing at her wedding. She took another long look, then released a heavy breath. In less than an hour she would be Mrs. London Brown.

"Bianca, are you okay?" Danica asked.

"Oh, please don't tell me you're about to get sick in your dress!"

She narrowed her eyes as Jessica Beaumont stepped into the room. "No, Mother. I'm not getting sick."

"Thank goodness," she said with relief. "Everybody is here."

"Mother Beaumont. She's just nervous. I was the same way when Jaden and I got married," Danica said.

Bianca looked over at Danica and gave her a warm smile. Only her feelings were nothing at all like those her sister-in-law had felt at her wedding. Danica and Jaden had been in love, looking forward to a life together. The deep, committed love they shared was evident in their actions. Anyone could see it in the way they talked, the way they couldn't keep their hands off each other. Relationships like that were few and far between. Danica had certainly made Jaden happy over the last two years. Whereas Bianca was nervous because she was having second thoughts about marrying a man for all the wrong reasons. She frowned because this wasn't at all the wedding she had hoped for, but, with a sigh, Bianca decided that she was going to have to make the best of it.

The colors of her wedding were beige and chocolate. Sheyna and a pregnant Danica looked gorgeous in strapless chocolate A-line dresses. While their niece, Arianna, was adorable in a cream-colored, floor-length flower-girl dress.

Sheyna came over to Bianca and started straightening her train. "You should see London. He is nervous as all get out."

Stunned, Bianca looked at Sheyna through the mirror and she nodded.

"His hands are shaking."

Bianca then dropped her eyes. For a moment, she thought that maybe he was truly nervous about them.

Brenna came over and took her hand. "You look so pretty." There were unshed tears in her eyes. "Wait until London sees you."

"Are you ready?" Debra asked.

"I guess so," Bianca answered, shaking inside as she looked

at her maid of honor, who was sexy in a chocolate two-tone slip dress that showcased every voluptuous curve.

Debra came over and gave her best friend a hug, trying not to ruin her makeup or wrinkle her dress. "Everything is going to work out. Just watch and see," she whispered for her ears only.

"I hope so," she said, glad someone knew how she was *really* feeling.

Debra released her with a smile. "I know so. The two of you look good together."

"Yes, you do." The others agreed.

"Grab your bouquets and let's go and take our places," Danica suggested and the others all followed her out of the room.

Bianca took one more look at herself, then swung around and found her mother still sitting on the chair looking stunning as ever in a taupe suit. She had a tissue in her hand and was dabbing tears from her eyes.

"You're going to make me ruin my makeup," she scolded.

Bianca smirked. "Then quit crying."

Jessica placed her hand over her heart and breathed deeply. "I'm not crying—just happy for you. Look at my little girl all grown up and you're getting married and getting ready to have a family. I'm losing my baby."

"Silly, I'm not going anywhere."

"When you have children, then you'll understand." She rose and walked over to where Bianca was standing and took a seat.

"I know you're rushing to marry him before you start showing and maybe it is sooner than you would have wanted, but I have a good feeling about London and I feel confident that everything is going to work out. I can feel it."

Her words meant the world to Bianca. "Thank you, Mother."

Her mother rose and joined her in front of the mirror. "Bianca, I love you. I might have a hard time showing it sometimes, but I want you to know that all I have cared about is your happiness."

Tears burned the backs of Bianca's eyes as she looked up at her mother. "Thanks, Mother. I love you, too." She hugged her until her mother gently pushed her away.

"Okay, enough of that. They're ready for you outside."

"I'll be out in a minute."

Her mother kissed her cheek and left Bianca alone.

Nervous, she sank onto a chair. What if she was making a mistake? She placed a protective hand against her stomach. "Sweetheart, Mama's doing this for you." She was doing this for her baby. She wanted her child to have a stable home. She had every intention of giving her child all her love. And maybe things would work out with her and London enough that he would be a wonderful father to her child even long after they had gone their separate ways.

"Bianca, I give you my word. I will be a father to your child no matter what."

She couldn't ask for anything more.

There was a knock, then the door opened and her father stepped in. Bianca rose and smiled. At sixty-two, her father still looked dashing in a black tuxedo.

"Don't you look mighty handsome?"

"It isn't every day a father gives away his only daughter." He gave her a warm hug, then took her hands and met her gaze. "I love you, Bianca. All I care about is your happiness. Are you sure this is what you want, because if it's not I'll sneak out the back door with you right now and we can hop a plane to the Bahamas by ourselves. I could use a little break from your mother."

She chuckled, then reached up and caressed her father's cheek. "That's why I love you so much. You've always kept Mother in line." Tears dampened her eyes. "No, I want to do this, Daddy." He gave her a big bear hug, then drew back. "Did I tell you how beautiful you look?"

She kissed his cheek.

"Ready?" he asked with tears in his eyes.

"Yes, but there's something I need to do first."

Chapter 19

"Man, relax, will you?" Mark said, and patted London lightly on the back.

How was he supposed to relax when in a few minutes he was going to be marrying Bianca Beaumont? London wondered. Just thinking about it made his hands sweat.

A tap on the door sent London's stomach down to the soles of his shoes. His shoulders tensed. It was time for everyone to take their places. Jaden went to see who it was.

Mark joined London, who was pacing in front of a pair of French doors. "You look like you're about to pass out. Too much partying last night," he teased.

Last night Jaden and a couple of their friends had thrown London a bachelor party at the Beaumont Hotel. Jaden was still pissed with him for betraying his trust, but he had come through for him last night, despite any ill feelings he may have still harbored. They had everything—food, liquor and exotic dancers. London couldn't explain it. Instead of enjoying himself, all he wanted to do was go over to Bianca's, curl up under the covers with her and hold her in his arms.

"Nah, just ready to get the formalities over with."

Mark nudged him with his elbow. "Yeah, right. You're ready to get that honeymoon started, huh? I ain't mad at you," he chuckled.

Jaden cleared his throat. "London, my sister would like to speak with you."

London's heart slammed against his chest. Bianca was at the door. Why? He wondered if she was having cold feet. He hoped not. They had already decided that this was the only way to protect the Beaumont name and to protect her baby from Collin. He reached the door just as Bianca stepped in.

"Sis, don't you know this is bad luck?" Jaden scowled as he smoothed the front of his tuxedo.

Bianca gave him a dismissive wave. "Be quiet. I need to speak to London."

London couldn't do anything but stare. Bianca looked…beautiful. Sexy as hell. He sucked in a sharp breath and took a giant mental step back. Every speck of moisture in his mouth vanished.

Her hair was in small spiral curls that were pulled back away from her perfectly round face. Her shoulders were bare and the floor-length dress molded her curves with a lover's attention to detail. His pulse drummed louder in his ears. Even though their wedding was a sham, he still considered himself lucky to be marrying such a beautiful woman.

He purposely cleared his throat. "Give us a minute," he said, and realized he sounded like a frog and cleared his throat again.

His cousin punched his shoulder. London pulled his gaze away from Bianca long enough to catch Mark winking just before heading out the door.

As soon as they were all gone, Bianca closed the door quietly behind them.

Her alluring and exotic scent wrapped around him and made him dizzy with longing. "You look incredible, Bianca."

A smile trembled on her lips. "Thank you. So do you."

He clenched his jaw and fought the unexpected and unwanted need snaking through his veins.

"Bianca, is everything all right?"

"Yes, I…" She lifted gaze and met his, and for a long moment neither of them said anything. Worry darkened her eyes and he had to fight the urge to kiss every worry line away from her forehead. "London, I wanted to thank you for everything you have done for me, but you don't have to do this. We don't have to get married. Drawing unwanted attention to me and my family no longer scares me."

The knot in his throat thickened. "Is that what you want?"

She hesitated. "I don't want you to have to change your lifestyle for me, and if you want to call this off—"

He laid a finger over her lips. She wasn't having second thoughts, but she thought he was. That's what he liked most about her. Her compassion and concern for others. That's the reason why they were getting married in the first place, because she was putting the needs of her family before her own.

His fingertips burned. He removed his finger from her soft mouth and reached down and clasped her hands in his.

"I get to spend the next year married to the sexiest woman in Sheraton Beach. How is that making a mistake?"

She bit her lower lip. "I just wanted to let you know that you don't have to do this if you don't want to. I'll survive and so will my family. We've been through a lot worse."

He pulled her closer. "I want to do this. You're starting to make me think that maybe you're the one who's having second thoughts."

She shook her head. "Absolutely not. Because at this point my mother would kill me if I did. Did you see all those people out there?"

He nodded. "I think the entire town closed down for business to be here," he said with a chuckle. "I guess we'd better give them something to talk about."

She gave a nervous laugh. "I guess so."

His gaze shifted to the bodice of her dress, which showed generous cleavage, and he found himself thinking about the chocolate color of her nipples and the weight of her breasts in his hands. They hadn't made love in over a week, but tonight all that would change. Tonight he would make love to his wife.

Bianca gave him one final look of uncertainty. "Are you sure?"

London pulled her into his arms. He pressed his lips to her forehead then pulled back. "I'm sure."

"If you change your mind—"

Before she could get it out, he lowered his mouth to hers, brushing his lips back and forth. Bianca brought her hands to his shoulders, holding on to him as he traced the shape of her mouth with his tongue. With a sigh, she opened her mouth and he teased her with his tongue, wanting to let her know that this was just a taste of what was yet to come. Tonight he was going to make her his. Finally, she placed a hand on his chest and pushed away. She stared up at him with her lips moist and parted.

"I'm not changing my mind," he reassured her. "Now go before I yank that gown from your body and make love to you right here, right now. To hell with all of those people waiting."

She must have seen that he was serious because she backed away and hurried out the door.

As soon as she was gone, London released a long breath as he moved to look out the window. Mark and the minister were outside waiting under a gazebo at the center of the magnificent rose garden.

It was showtime. Struggling to breathe, he turned on his heel.

Reaching for the brass handles, he opened the French doors and strolled over to his assigned place next to his cousin. His eyes traveled over to the several hundred people sitting under the cool shaded trees, waiting for the wedding to begin. His sisters waved from the second row. Waving back, he gave them a wide grin. They were happy for him.

Things were not going to change. He and Bianca would share a home and he would have a companion in his bed for the next year. And when the time came, they would both go their separate ways. Although he had every intention of being a permanent part of her child's life.

"Is everything okay?" Mark asked.

"Yes, everything is fine," he said.

"For a minute there I thought maybe she had come to her senses and wanted a real man like me."

London ignored his cousin's wisecracks, clasped his hands in front, fixed his gaze on the opposite end of the aisle and waited.

Jabarie escorted Bianca's mother down the aisle. She took her seat upfront and gave London a sweet welcoming smile. His belly knotted. She trusted him with her daughter. And he wouldn't let her down.

From the corner of the garden a harpist plucked out a tune. His talented sister, Denise, stood off to the side with a cordless microphone in hand as she sang Stevie Wonder's "Ribbon in the Sky."

The double French doors leading from the main part of the house opened and one by one the wedding party came out. A grin curled his lips when Brenna and Jabarie's three-year-old daughter came down the aisle carrying a small basket of flowers. Arianna scattered rose petals randomly as she made her way up the aisle. When she reached the end she rushed to sit on her grandmother's lap.

The music changed to the wedding march and London breathed in admiration as he caught sight of Bianca floating regally toward him on the arm of her father. The tie knotted at his throat threatened to choke him. For the hundredth time he was overcome by his desire for her. Sunlight, soon to set into dusk, danced on her curls and sparkled on the beading of her dress. He squared his shoulders and awaited his bride.

On the verge of hyperventilating, Bianca struggled to regulate her breathing and then she met London's gaze across the garden and forgot about breathing altogether.

The strength in London's gaze drew her forward as surely as her father's firm grip on her elbow, guiding her down the aisle. Not once did her eyes leave London's. She took in his attire. London was mainly a khakis and polo shirt man, yet this afternoon, he wore a finely tailored tuxedo, as if he had been born to wear one. In fact, he looked handsome and downright dangerous. His good looks were enough to bring any woman to her knees, and today she was no exception.

When she reached the end of the short aisle, he held out his hand. Everything is going to be all right, his steady brown gaze seemed to tell her. Her father released her, kissed her cheek and stepped away. London took his place beside her. His warm fingers curled around hers and a sense of calmness settled over her.

The minister began the traditional service Bianca had heard many times before. The familiar words eased the tension that gripped her stomach. London eased a simple gold band on her finger and repeated his vows in a firm, confident voice. When it was Bianca's turn to say her vows, her voice trembled and when she finally slid the wide gold band over London's knuckle, she gasped. It was officially too late to change her mind.

"I now pronounce you husband and wife." The minister closed his prayer book and beamed. "London, you may kiss your bride."

Bianca met his eyes. He smiled at her and he leaned in close. Her heart stumbled then raced. His hands curved over her bare shoulders and his long fingers sent a heated rush over her body. She dampened her lips. She thought she saw a flare of something besides lust before London bent his head, but he lowered his lids before she could identify the emotion. Bianca leaned into him, resting her hands against his strong body. She felt safe and in danger at the same time.

His mouth opened over hers. The world around them disappeared. The flick of his tongue on her bottom lip struck her with the charge of a lightning bolt, and then he tasted her. She couldn't help but taste him back. *Delicious.* Her hands slid up his neck. She tunneled her fingers through his hair. His palms eased down over the slick fabric of her gown, pulling her firmly against his body and deepening the kiss.

Loud applause and laughter penetrated the sensual fog. London slowly lifted his head. Bianca stared up at him for a long intense moment, and she realized that if she weren't careful, she would definitely be in danger of losing her heart.

"Ladies and gentleman, allow me to be the first to introduce Mr. and Mrs. London Brown."

The photographer moved in close and the flash went off in her face. Blinking rapidly, Bianca pasted on what she hoped looked like a blissful smile while inside her world had just been turned every which way.

She was only vaguely aware of her surroundings, of Debra hugging her tightly, and Mona and Denise with tears in their eyes, kissing her on the cheek. "My brother could not have made a better choice," Denise said. Clarence kissed Bianca and shook his son's hand as he congratulated them both.

Finally, Jessica turned to their guests. "Please join us on the patio for cocktails," she said in her best hostess voice.

Chapter 20

The wedding. The kiss. The announcement that Bianca was now his wife hit London hard. He couldn't take his eyes off her.

My wife.

He watched her all during dinner and the cutting of the cake. Now the deejay had slowed down the music and he was moving across the patio to claim her.

"Sweetheart, can I have this dance?"

Bianca smiled up at him, then offered him her hand, and he escorted her out onto the dance floor. Instantly, he pulled her against him and she locked her arms around his neck.

"I think everything went quite well," she said as she followed his lead.

"No, things went better than well." Their marriage was supposed to be temporary, him helping a friend. End of story. Only he wanted more...after the small ceremony, he wanted a lot more.

"Hey, what's going on in that head of yours?" Bianca asked, getting his attention.

London gazed down at her smiling face, then seared her mouth with a long, passionate kiss. "You. I can't stop thinking about you," he murmured, then pressed his lips to hers again. When he finally came up for air, he held her tightly against his beating heart. "Do you feel that? That's how you make me feel."

She leaned back and stared up at his face, seeing how serious he really was. Her eyes grew large and round, filled with surprise. "I don't know what to say."

"Say that as soon as this song is over you'll be ready to sneak out the back door."

Her lips curled in a smile that challenged his libido. "I'll meet you in the limo."

Half an hour later, London unlocked the front door and shoved it open. He swept Bianca up in his arms. She gasped, squirmed and kicked her feet. He tightened his hold. "Hold still before I drop you," he whispered against her ear.

She giggled and wound her arms around his neck. "Will you put me down?"

"Not until we're inside." London stepped inside and kicked the door closed, then slowly lowered her to her feet and immediately brought his mouth to hers. He couldn't get enough of her.

He took her hand. "Well? What do you think?"

Bianca tore her eyes from him and suddenly realized that she was in London's home, now their home, for the first time in over a week. She glanced around, eyes wide.

"Oh, my goodness! When did you have time to do all this?"

"I hired a crew to have it ready in time for our wedding."

"It's beautiful!" She threw her arms around his neck and pressed her lips to his. When she had insisted that it was a waste of time for him to sell his home, since their marriage was only going to last for a year, he got her to agree to move in with him. However, Bianca had hinted that the house lacked warmth and femininity and she was going to make some changes after she moved in. Refusing to let his pregnant wife lift so much as a paintbrush, London had hired a crew to renovate his house in seven days.

"It's my gift to you. I want you to feel like this is your home."

"Thanks to you, I already do." Rising onto her tiptoes she pressed her lips to his. London groaned then swung her into his arms and carried her down the hall.

"Where are we going?"

"To bed. You can look at the rest of the house later. Right now, I need to make love to my wife."

As soon as they were in his room, he lowered her onto her feet. Bianca pushed away and walked around the room, admiring the eggshell walls, the plush cream carpet and the large bed that was set high off the floor. On the wall above the bed was a sunset beach scene of deep rich colors painted across a large canvas.

"That painting is gorgeous," she said with admiration.

He swiveled his head to look at her. "The moment I saw it I thought of you."

While she looked around at the decor and rich, new furnishings, he slipped out of his tuxedo jacket and loosened his tie. "I've been dying to do that all day," he said after blowing out a long breath. Bianca hadn't heard a word he said. She stood at the center of the room still shaking her head with disbelief. "Baby, you okay?"

She swung around. "London, I can't believe you did all this. Everything is exactly the way I would have wanted it."

He tossed his shirt over onto a cream-colored upholstered chair in front of a large picture window, then moved beside her and slipped his arm around her waist. "I'll have to admit, I couldn't have pulled it off without my sisters' help."

"I'll have to thank them personally."

"Later. Right now we've got business to attend to." He lowered his mouth to hers and slipped his tongue inside, giving her a sample of what was yet to come. She pressed her hands to his chest and leaned into the kiss, giving as good as he gave.

"Tonight will be the first time I make love to you as my wife," he whispered against her lips. Calling her his wife sounded so right.

Bianca's hand slid along the hard ridges of his abdomen down to the narrow patch of hair leading downward. She eased her hand lower still over the erection that strained against the fly of his pants.

"Well, well. What do we have here?" she asked with a hint of mischief in her eyes.

London's head fell back and he let out a low groan. She smiled as she slid her hand over the full hard length of him.

"Bianca," he whispered hoarsely as his hand closed over hers and stilled it. "Don't."

She leaned into him, pressing her breasts against him and whispered, "Why not?"

"Because if you don't stop it's going to be over before it gets started and that is not the type of wedding night I had planned for us." He moved her hands behind her back with one hand and unzipped her dress with the other, then watched it fall to the floor. Bianca immediately kicked it away. His gaze turned smoldering and hot as he eyed her thong panties and the garters holding her thigh-high stockings in place. London pulled her against him. With a wicked smile on her lips she pushed him back on the bed then climbed on top and straddled him.

Leaning forward, she pressed her breasts to his chest, then rocked gently against his erection and his grip on her hips tightened. His hot mouth grazed her throat as she whispered in his ear. "You want me?"

"You know I do," he growled against her cheek.

London's hands roamed her body up her back then down over her hips and back to her shoulders. His fingers twisted in the straps of her bra. He eased the straps down, leaving her breasts exposed to him. Desire flashed in his dark eyes. He bent his head to her and his tongue glided over a nipple, causing it to pebble tightly.

Her breath caught. He gave her no time to recover from his touch. His hands cupped her breasts and kneaded them gently. His tongue flicked the other nipple and it puckered to an almost painful point.

She gasped as the pleasure built deep inside. Her fingers gripped his steel biceps. She looked down at him as he laved and sucked her taut peaks.

One hand left her breast and eased up the outer side of her thigh. He touched the exposed skin above the lacy top of her stocking and expertly unfastened the garter with a quick flick. While doing so, his fingers grazed the damp crotch of her panties.

She flinched and London groaned loudly at her reaction. He released her nipple and allowed his tongue to run along her neck and cheek before meeting her lips.

Bianca was almost breathless. Her insides hummed. Her temples pulsed. She was hot and turned on beyond words.

"London," she urged, desperately needing him to touch her. "Please."

He kissed her again. His lips and tongue tangled with hers. As he deepened their kiss, his finger pushed aside the material between her legs and brushed over the wet flesh.

Bianca broke the kiss and gasped. Sharp stabs of desire pierced her deep inside. Her hard nipples grazed his skin as she fought for a full, steady breath.

London stroked her until she was panting in his ear. She rose up a bit off his lap, giving him better access. He found that precious nub and rubbed it slowly, intensifying the throbbing. Bianca closed her eyes and her lips parted slightly as a sigh of lust and longing passed through them.

Then his fingers slid inside her and she cried out, her body responding fervently to the sudden, sweet intrusion. The pressure inside her mounted to an unbearable degree as he took her to the brink. But she wanted more than this. She wanted all of him.

"Don't you want to be inside me, London?" she asked on a labored breath.

"You know I do, baby,"

She reached for his hand, removed his fingers and unfastened his belt. She unzipped his pants and slid them below his hips. The tip of his hard penis strained above the waistband of his sexy black briefs. Her fingers skimmed over the smooth skin and he bucked beneath her touch. She pushed the briefs down, then her hand wrapped around his thick shaft.

She eased her body over the head of his cock and rubbed it against her wet flesh. London groaned. His chest rose and fell sharply with his quick breath. Bianca slowly drew him into her body, one exquisitely sensual inch at a time. His hands cupped her breasts and his thumbs teased her nipples. She took him in farther, then eased back, drawing him out of her. She repeated this motion over and over until he gave a low primal groan.

Finally, Bianca drew him completely inside her and rocked against him. When she knew they were both close, she increased the tempo, riding him hard and fast. His hands grabbed at her hips, and he pressed her down onto him as he arched upward, meeting her strokes and thrusting deeper and deeper inside her.

"I'm going to come, baby," he said on a harsh breath.

"Yes, London. Now!"

His hands slid to her bottom and he cupped her cheeks. He pushed himself into her and he felt her body shake just before he convulsed with an orgasm.

Moments later, a shattering climax rocked her body and she cried out. She squeezed her inner muscles tightly around him. He desperately wanted to prolong the sensations rioting inside his body for as long as possible, because their time together would only be temporary.

Chapter 21

Bianca stared out the window of the airplane for the third time. "London, where are we going?" she asked, burning with curiosity.

He looked up from his newspaper. "You'll find out soon enough. Now come back over and sit down." He chuckled silently at her persistence. He had chartered a plane to keep their honeymoon location a surprise.

Returning to her seat, Bianca gave a frustrated groan. They were on their honeymoon and she had no idea where in the world they were going. All London had allowed her to pack was a toothbrush.

"London, please tell me where we're going." She snatched his paper and tossed it aside then moved over to his lap. "Please," she whined.

He groaned. Having her that close was hazardous to his libido. "I guess it doesn't matter now."

She started planting quick, persuasive kisses all along his face. "Then tell me. Where are we going?"

Turning his face, he planted a kiss on her lips, then tipped his head back and looked at her. "To Grand Turk Island, in the Turks and Caicos."

Her eyes grew large and round. "I've never been there."

"I know." When her brows rose, he added, "I asked Jabarie." Reaching up, he caressed her cheek. "I wanted to take you somewhere you'd never been before."

"Oh, I've been to Jamaica and the Bahamas, but never the Turks and Caicos Islands. Oooh, how exciting!"

He laced her fingers with his, loving how small they appeared next to his. "Did you know the island is only seven square miles and has fewer than four thousand residents?"

"No, I didn't."

"Well, it's true. And do you know what that means?"

Bianca shook her head, not following him at all. "No."

London studied her face for a long time. "It means I get to have you all to myself."

She gave him a smile that made his most intimate part ache. Leaning forward, he caught her lips in a kiss that was deep and demanding. The sound of her faint little moan made his heart pound and his body hum with the anticipation of making love to her the first chance he got.

The plane landed. A driver was there waiting for them. As they drove along the island, London watched Bianca's expressions in amusement. She was fascinated by everything she saw as she listened to the driver giving her the history of the island. London knew she would like it here. Two years ago Grand Turk had found a place in his heart. The island, known for its colorful British colonial architecture, exuded its own distinct Caribbean charm and Bianca clearly savored it as much as he did.

It wasn't long before they pulled in front of a private Caribbean home on a cul-de-sac. Bianca found the spacious tropical home gorgeous. After a quick tour of the downstairs, she moved to the living room. Standing near a large window, she stared off at the beach paradise blessed with crystal-clear, turquoise waters and smooth white beaches.

London came behind her and pulled her to him. "You like what you see?"

She turned in his arms. "I love it! Thank you so much for bringing me here."

"That's what friends are for, right?"

Her smile widened. "Right."

"Why don't we get changed and go spend some time on the beach?"

She frowned. "Sounds wonderful, but I don't have anything to wear. Remember, you refused to let me pack a suitcase."

He gave her a slow grin. "Come with me." London took Bianca's hand and led her up a spiral staircase to the master suite at the end of the hallway. Inside was a massive bed covered in a Caribbean-printed bedspread. The furniture was made of rich, dark woods. The oak floor was sparingly covered with mosaic-printed rugs. The blinds were open wide, displaying a large picture window and a beautiful view of the beach below.

He watched her staring outside in awe. One would think Bianca was a small-town girl who had never left Sheraton Beach. He knew for a fact that she had visited over thirteen different countries—one for every other year of her life.

"Check out the closets."

With an amused look, Bianca practically skipped over and slid the closet door to the left. She stared inside, then looked over at him, again with a narrowed frown. "Who do these clothes belong to?" she demanded.

Chuckling, he briefly closed his eyes before looking into her angry eyes.

"Well, I'm waiting," she said with an impatient hand on her hip.

He walked over to her, trying to contain his amusement. "The clothes belong to my sisters. I'm sure there's a swimsuit inside that's never been worn."

She looked confused and relieved at the same time. "This house belongs to your family?"

He nodded. "My sisters and I bought it about a year ago."

"How wonderful. My parents own property in California and Florida, but nothing like this."

London draped an arm across her shoulders. She closed her arms around him and, tipping her head back, her lips grazed his chin.

"You were jealous?" he said before she kissed him again.

"I was not," she denied.

"Yes, you were. I think you care more about me than you want to admit."

She pushed away and winked. "I'm not admitting anything. We have an agreement and I'm going to live up to my end of it. That means enjoying everything that this year will bring without expecting anything more than it really is. Now let's get dressed and have some fun."

Bianca turned her back to him and looked through the closet until she found a bikini her size with the price tag still on.

His heart was pounding heavily in his chest. The attraction was so strong and he knew Bianca felt it, too. London watched her from behind as she stepped across the hall into the bathroom and shook his head.

That woman is going to be the death of me.

They spent the afternoon riding around the small town, admiring large homes and touring an old prison. Later, after a scrumptious dinner of conch and rice and peas, Bianca changed from the sundress she had been wearing into swim gear. Together they took the path leading away from the house down onto the private beach. They swam and enjoyed each other's company while the scent of the ocean whipped around their bodies. London couldn't take his eyes off her in the two-piece fuchsia bikini she'd chosen. She was standing, looking out on the ocean with her back to him. His gaze traveled up the length of her shapely legs and perfect butt with male appreciation.

His wife was beautiful beyond words.

His wife. That had a lovely ring to it. He wasn't sure if he'd ever get used to hearing those words. London quietly moved up behind her. Reaching around, he found the ties to her top and pulled them loose, then cupped her bare breasts with his hands. She gasped on contact but didn't pull away. Instead, she leaned back, pressing her body against his. He massaged her breasts, flicking her nipples until she gasped with pleasure.

His hands were hot on her skin, making her wild with wanting. Turning around, Bianca pressed her bare breasts against his chest, the fine hairs grazing her sensitive nipples. When he shoved her bikini bottom down to her ankles and tossed them aside she was more than willing to accept what he had to offer. She watched as he lowered his swim trunks and kicked them away.

"Lie down," he ordered softly.

Obeying, she lowered herself onto the large blue beach blanket with her legs spread, and London knelt between her parted thighs. He then stroked her inner thighs and she didn't pull away as he eased a finger inside her wet folds. He pushed in and out slowly, and when she began to rock her hips against him, meeting each thrust, he increased the rate.

Knowing they were outside on a private beach, about to make love where any beachcombers could see them if they really wanted to, had her burning with wicked desire.

"Please," she begged, "make love to me."

She didn't have to ask twice. Gripping her hips, London guided his length into her moist entrance. She gasped, then squeezed him like they were meant to be together—forever. Only they weren't. At least she wasn't going to be foolish enough to believe that. Never again. It is what it is, she reminded herself. She planned to enjoy every second they had.

"Yes," she moaned.

London withdrew to the tip then pushed forward again. She cried out, her breath coming in little pants.

He plunged again and again, and she cried out with each thrust, loving the way he felt inside her. She was his, and he was hers—even if it was just for the moment.

Finally, she came. She gripped and milked him before she collapsed around him. He continued to pump into her, filling her with everything he had and came shortly after. As soon as their heart rates returned to normal, London rose with her in his arms and carried her into the house and back to bed.

Chapter 22

Bianca lifted London's arm, which was draped protectively around her waist, and carefully slid out from beneath him.

On her tiptoes, she moved across the room, thankful that her steps were silenced by the plush carpet. As soon as she was inside the bathroom, she shut the door, moved over to a vanity in the corner and took a seat. With her shoulders slumped forward she shook her head and wondered what she was going to do. She had done everything she could to keep it from happening. Denying her feelings. Reminding herself that it was only a deal. Not spending any more time with him than necessary. Yet none of that had made a difference. Some way, somehow London had wiggled his way past the barrier that guarded her heart.

She had fallen in love with her husband.

Bianca lowered her head and brought her hands to her forehead, then groaned. This was not at all how she had planned it.

Utterly surprised, she had discovered how alike she and London were. They enjoyed the same R&B music, loved to read and had business minds that worked well together. The time she had spent working on the marketing for his restaurants and the input he had given had proven that. He cooked. She cleaned. They laughed together and their sex life was phenomenal.

She had accepted Collin's marriage proposal, knowing deep in her heart that she didn't love him as a woman should love the man she was about to marry. Sure, she enjoyed being with him, but she had not wholly given herself to him. His kisses were nice, but her body hadn't reacted the same way it had when London made love to her.

Now she knew what love was.

The realization hit her hard and she shuddered. *What in the world was she going to do?*

The sun had begun to rise. Tangled in the sheets, London lay on his side. He stared down at the beautiful woman sleeping comfortably beside him.

His wife.

He couldn't seem to tear his eyes away from her. To him, Bianca Beaumont Brown was beautiful. So beautiful he could not put his emotions into words. He'd never felt his heart pound so hard from doing something more than just staring at a woman.

What was happening to him? Better yet, why was it happening? Bianca made it perfectly clear that falling in love with him was out of the question. Yet a part of him wished that they were married for real.

She gave a soft moan and the innocent expression on her face brought a smile to London's lips. He leaned down and gave her a delicate kiss on the forehead. He kissed her again, and this time she mumbled something that he couldn't decipher. When she snuggled closer, he realized there was no way he was ever letting her go. He would just have to show her how good they were together, so that she couldn't imagine her life without him.

Chapter 23

Bianca heard a knock near her open door. "Come in," she called out.

Debra stuck her head inside her office door. "I see you're back."

Lowering the pencil, she folded her hands on the desk and smiled. "Yes, I am."

She pursed her lips with disapproval. "I guess I'm the last to know, since you've been ignoring all of my phone calls."

"Not *all* of them. I was planning to call you this morning."

"Uh-huh," Debra said, looking unconvinced as she stepped into Bianca's office wearing a slamming peach designer suit.

Bianca gasped. "Oh, my! I love your new hairstyle."

Grinning, Debra combed her fingers through her short, spiked hair. "Thank you, girl. I felt I was do for a change. After seeing you going down the aisle, I decided that maybe it's time for me to find myself a new man."

Bianca's brows rose. "Really?"

"Yes. At least for an hour or two." Debra's eyes crinkled as they shared the fun. With a wave of her hand, she dismissed their laughter. "Okay, enough with the stalling. I want to hear all about your honeymoon." Debra flopped down in the chair across from her, an expectant look on her face.

Bianca grinned. "Fabulous." Her pulse began to race just at the thought. She told Debra about the last four days she'd spent snorkeling, swimming, walking along the shore holding hands and the numerous hours she'd spent lying in London's arms as he took his time making love to her.

"Damn, girl!" Debra studied Bianca intently and said, "Are you in love yet?"

Bianca met Debra's gaze, no longer denying the truth. "Yes, I think I am."

Debra practically jumped out her chair. "I knew it. And what did he say when you told him?"

Dropping her eyes to the report on her desk, Bianca shook her head. "I didn't tell him."

"Are you crazy? Why the hell not?"

Bianca looked up, then shrugged. "Because we have an agreement, and falling in love isn't part of it."

"Maybe not in the beginning, but a lot has changed between the two of you. You're married, living in the same house, getting ready to have a baby. If that isn't a lot of change, I don't know what is."

Debra just didn't know how much she wished that was true. But it could never happen because she wouldn't allow it to. She had risked her heart once and look where it got her.

"But we both knew the rules from day one. He agreed to give my baby a name and that is exactly what London has done for me, and I love him for it."

"But what about forgetting about what the two of you agreed on and taking a chance on loving each other?"

Oh, it definitely sounded good, yet everything that sounded good wasn't always good for you, Bianca thought.

"No. You know what they say, if it ain't broke, don't fix it. Our relationship is perfect just the way it is," Bianca said out loud.

"It sounds like it's broke to me."

Yes, Bianca had to agree. However, she wasn't prepared to do anything about it.

* * *

There was enough going on at the new restaurant to keep London fully occupied. Even with a manager and a staff, there were still plenty of things left to be done for the grand opening this weekend. However, trying to prepare for the big night with Bianca swirling around in his mind was not making his job easy.

He took his job seriously, yet Bianca was the first woman who ever distracted him from his work. He couldn't take a breath without smelling her scent or remembering her smile.

He knew from the beginning that their marriage was simply a business arrangement so why couldn't he get his heart to coop-erate? Bianca was not interested in forever. She had made that point perfectly clear on several occasions. So why did his heart refuse to listen?

Leaning back in his chair, he swung around and looked out the wide window, staring out at the bustling downtown. He already missed the smell of the ocean and the magnificent view from their bedroom window. Usually, he was excited about the restaurant and his growing success. He enjoyed the hell out of his job. But now that he had Bianca in his life, none of that seemed anywhere near as important as her and the baby.

Now he wanted what he thought he would find time for later. He wanted a family. Not just any family. *His family.* Bianca and the baby. He wanted her permanently in his life.

But she doesn't want you.

With a scowl, he turned away from the window. He had every intention of keeping her in his life—permanently.

Chapter 24

Over the next week, they settled into a routine. The grand opening was drawing closer with every passing day, so London stayed in a hotel in New Castle. There were so many last-minute details that Bianca was amazed at how well London managed everything.

He was a natural.

Bianca played hooky from work and accompanied him. The restaurant was twice the size of the one in Sheraton Beach, but it had the same down-home feeling and warmth, and had the same aroma Mama's kitchen was supposed to.

Bianca chuckled at that thought. Not *her* mother's kitchen.

Memorial Day came and went and the big day was finally upon them.

Glancing around the restaurant at the tables that were all full, she smiled. This night was everything London had hoped for.

She'd hired a local, old-school band to perform. The music added to the comfortable vibe the restaurant exuded.

Playing hostess, Bianca made the rounds, spoke to customers and offered to help with anything anyone needed, while her husband worked the kitchen, making sure everything was running smoothly. Every time London stepped out onto the floor, Bianca knew it because her body got tingly and hot.

The last few weeks had been fabulous. The more time they spent together and the more they got to know each other, the more her protective layers began to fall away. Bianca had not known it was possible to feel so comfortable and fulfilled in a relationship.

And she was terrified.

Her days and nights were spent in the company of a man who made her laugh one minute and cry out in ecstasy the next. He taught her things in bed that she had only read about in erotic novels, yet each and every time London made her feel like the sexiest woman alive.

Deep down she never wanted this wonderful feeling to end. However, even though he spent every night beside her, London never mentioned a commitment or life after the baby. Bianca tried to convince herself to live for the moment and then worry about the rest when it happened.

She moved to the side of the room and glanced around at the happy faces. London had worked hard to pull the night off, and she felt a stir of admiration for him. Her eyes followed him as he greeted the crowd, said a few words, laughed with a child and patted the hand of an elderly woman. All around her, people were laughing, talking, eating or licking their fingers. The wait staff rushed around the floor, yet Bianca barely noticed. She only had eyes for London.

"Isn't this wonderful?" said someone to her right.

Bianca looked over at Mona, who was running the carryout counter.

"I've barely had five minutes to breathe. The phones have been ringing nonstop!" she added, eyes sparkling with excitement. "Dad is so proud." The phone rang, and she answered it immediately while Bianca looked to her left where London's father and the twins sat watching the crowd. Clarence had been smiling and dabbing his eyes all evening. A lump rose in her throat. Her father-in-law looked almost as happy as he had when she and London invited him to their house for Memorial Day and announced that they were expecting a baby. This would be his first grandchild.

It warmed Bianca's heart. Her baby was going to have two parents, grandparents and a whole lot of love.

Speaking of love…her eyes moved across the room to London, who was personally delivering a tray of food to a large table.

"You really love my brother, don't you?"

Tearing her eyes from London, she found Mona resting her elbows on the counter, smiling knowingly.

Embarrassed, Bianca dropped her eyes. "Is it that obvious?"

Mona reached over and squeezed her shoulder. "Yes, you can't seem to take your eyes off him, but he's the same way with you. Girl, I'm so happy for the two of you and you just don't know how happy I was when Dad told me about the baby. I can't wait to hold my nephew in my arms."

Bianca frowned. "Nephew, uh-uh. We're having a girl."

Mona shook her head. "We've got enough women in our family."

"And we have too many big-head boys in mine."

They shared a laugh.

The phone rang again. While Mona went back to work, Bianca shifted her gaze back to the man who was driving her insane. Needing to be near him, she glided across the room and got excited when he noticed her coming. London grinned, took her hand and guided her into the kitchen.

"Hey."

"Hi," she replied, shyly. "Looks like you're a big hit."

He grinned. "Seems that way."

"Your dad looks pleased," Bianca said softly, unable to take her eyes off London.

His smile widened. "Yes, he is. He's already talking about finding a location in Wilmington."

"That's wonderful."

"No, *you're* wonderful. Thanks for all your help. I could not have done this without you."

"There was no other place I'd rather be." When he held her tightly in his arms, she closed her eyes. What she'd said wasn't completely true. There was one place she would prefer to be and that was solidly ensconced in London's heart.

Chapter 25

Bianca looked over the marketing plan once more and a smile curled her lips. What she had proposed would put her husband's family restaurant on the map. Two weeks ago at the grand opening, London had mentioned that his father was looking for a location in Wilmington, and she knew just the place—Kaonis Kitchen.

Her cousin, Diamere, had saved his father's restaurant from bankruptcy and was doing a fabulous job of keeping it going. The three J's had given him a business loan, and early this year Diamere had paid them back with interest. But after his father passed away six months ago, Diamere decided that he was ready to sell, so he could concentrate his time and energy on a couple of nightclubs he'd bought last year in Philadelphia. The restaurant was in a prime location in central Delaware and needed someone who had a passion for the restaurant business. And that's where London came in. Bianca smiled as recalled the conversation they'd had the night before about him purchasing Kaonis Kitchen. His face had lit up like the face of a child with a new toy.

In the last several weeks, Bianca had become very involved in his family business with the recent opening of his second restaurant. She'd even offered to invest in the restaurant. London and his father had agreed. Now that Bianca was part owner of the business, Diamere was more than happy to sell, because he'd be keeping the restaurant in the family.

Family. That was Bianca, London and the baby. A family. It was something she didn't think she wanted, but now she knew that she did. As much as it scared her, she wanted London permanently in her life.

She pursed her lips thoughtfully. Last night London had made love to her until early morning and she thought she was going to cry. He held her in his arms and stroked her stomach and talked about their future with their baby girl. What more could she possibly hope for?

"You look happy."

Bianca glanced up at the door to see Jaden leaning in the doorway. "Did you expect any less?"

Staring at her, he hesitated before saying, "To be honest, I didn't know what to expect. The engagement was a surprise. The baby an even bigger one. I didn't even know the two of you were dating."

She leaned across her desk with her arms on the table. "No one knew."

Jaden shrugged and moved forward into her office with his hands in his pockets. "I'm cool with it now and respect that he's your husband, but I'm still feeling pissed off that my boy went behind my back and was messing with my sister."

"It happens like that sometimes, Jaden. We can't control who we fall in love with."

He smirked. "So you're saying you love him?"

Bianca answered without hesitation. "Yes, Jaden, I do."

"Then I guess I need to be happy for you."

"I'd appreciate it if you would be."

There was a moment of silence. She didn't know if it was because he was having a hard time accepting that his sister had grown up or that she had married his best friend. She pondered a thought for a moment before making a decision and reached inside her bottom desk drawer and pulled out a large yellow envelope.

"Let me show you something." She slid the envelope across the desk and watched as Jaden looked through the contents inside.

He gave her a puzzled look. "Who *is* this cat?"

"That is Collin, my baby's real daddy."

He looked even more confused.

"You hired London to spy on my fiancé. Well that's my fiancé, or at least he was until London brought this report to me. And instead of my tarnishing the family name by raising a child out of wedlock, he offered to marry me. To keep my baby away from Collin, who, as it turns out, is only interested in the Beaumont money."

Jaden was speechless.

"Do Mother and Dad know about this?"

"Of course not and as far as I'm concerned no one else needs to know. The only reason I told you was because I couldn't stand seeing you questioning your friendship with London when all he did was act like a friend to you by protecting your little sister." From the look on his face, she knew she had hit home.

"Damn!" Jaden shook his head. "Can you ever forgive me?"

"You're my brother. I don't have a choice but to forgive you. But the person you need to be talking to is my husband."

"Yeah, I guess I do." He rose. "Thanks, sis."

She came around and gave him a big hug. "I love you, big head."

"I love you, too."

She watched him leave, then reached for the phone. She suddenly had the strong urge to hear her husband's voice.

Much later, in bed, Bianca lay in London's arms after another round of sizzling lovemaking. He pulled her close, his hands resting protectively on her growing stomach.

"Bianca, we need to talk."

Something in the tone of his voice caused her to stiffen. She had a sinking feeling that she wasn't going to like what he was about to say. But she shouldn't have been surprised. All evening London had behaved strangely distant until she had curled onto his lap after dinner and kissed him. It was then he behaved as if his resistance had lifted. Apparently, it was only temporary.

She swallowed the lump in her throat "About what?"

"Us and these last several weeks."

Bianca rolled onto her back, then dropped her gaze to his chest so he wouldn't read the disappointment. The comforting strokes did nothing to ease the sadness settling in her chest. She should have known the last few weeks were too good to be true. Sure enough, London was getting ready to remind her that their marriage was strictly a business arrangement—she was certain of that. There was no way she could take another blow. After Collin she simply couldn't sustain another disappointment. She couldn't be rejected again.

Taking a deep breath, she lifted her eyes to him, then scrambled up to a sitting position, determined to say what she had to say before he did. "Before you say anything, I just want you to know that I have enjoyed these last few weeks together. I have experienced things that I have never felt before and I thank you for it. But we need to remember that our marriage isn't real and I'm not looking for commitment. I get the feeling these last couple of weeks that you have forgotten that."

He gave her a long, hard stare. "I haven't forgotten anything. I just don't see anything wrong with us enjoying each other while it lasts." His voice was nonchalant. His words hurt far worse than a slap.

Somehow she managed to swallow the lump in her throat. "Yes. Well, maybe we need to tone that down a notch." Because it hurt too much to be with the man she loved, knowing he didn't love her back.

It took him a long time to speak. London squeezed her tightly in his arms. "Sure. No problem. Now get some rest."

She forced the tears from her voice. "Okay."

Long after she had drifted off to sleep, London held her in his arms. He never wanted to release her. The conversation didn't go nearly as he had planned. He had intended to tell her that he was feeling something he had never felt before and that he loved her. That he hadn't tried to fall in love, yet it had happened. Instead, Bianca had put the brakes on things and quickly reminded him that their relationship was nothing more than an arrangement for the sake of her unborn child.

In so many words, Bianca had made it clear that as soon as a

year had passed their relationship would be over. London felt like
the wind had been knocked out of his lungs. And even though
he was still holding her in his arms, he suddenly felt all alone.

Chapter 26

"Dinner's ready," Bianca announced late one evening.

London jumped at the sound of her voice. If Bianca noticed, she didn't say anything. "Just give me a minute to wash my hands," he said.

London soaped his hands, staring at himself over the bathroom mirror as he did so. He was scowling, and he knew why. The last week had been close to impossible. The wall between them now was so thick that he couldn't push pass it; he had pulled back, as well. He tried to convince himself that maybe it was for the best. That the best thing to do was to follow the terms of their agreement and quit trying to make their marriage something it was never intended to be. He should be flattered that Bianca wasn't trying to shackle him down and that in less than a year he would be back on the single circuit.

As he reached for a towel, he frowned. Single life no longer appealed to him. He was happier with Bianca than he had ever been when he was juggling women and appointment books. Nope, nothing had changed. He still wanted Bianca. Besides, he was a Brown. And none of them would ever be called quitters.

He would just have to slowly wiggle his way around that barrier and hopefully, by the time the baby arrived, everything would be as it should.

When he returned he found Bianca sitting quietly at the table, waiting for him. The lasagna she had prepared looked appetizing, as did the large tossed salad and garlic bread. "I wish you hadn't gone to so much trouble," he said, taking his seat at the opposite end of the table. "I'd planned to go get Chinese or something."

She looked up. "I know. I thought you'd enjoy a home-cooked meal. And—" she shrugged "—I thought I'd give it a try."

He managed to say the wrong thing and now she was apologizing. "I wasn't complaining. I just didn't know you…"

"Could cook?" she asked, then gave a soft chuckle. "I can't. Not really. Sheyna helped me make the lasagna. All I had to do was bring it home and pop it in the oven. The salad I learned how to make when I was a kid. When my mother wasn't looking, I would sneak in the kitchen and help our cook."

Nodding, London took a bite of the meaty lasagna. It was just the way he liked it, with Italian sausage. "Everything tastes great," he said at last.

They ate mostly in silence. London tried to think of something to say. They talked a little about how well the new restaurant was doing and his plan to meet with her cousin, Diamere, tomorrow. When they both pushed their plates away, London rose. "The least I can do is the dishes. Go and take a long hot bath."

Bianca gave him a weary smile. "That sounds like a good idea."

By the time she climbed from her hot bath, Bianca felt renewed and reinvigorated. The hot water had calmed her nerves but did nothing to ease the pain in her heart. She loved London, yet she didn't have a clue how to tell him how much he was coming to mean to her. The last few days they had been walking around each other, both feeling on edge, and she just wasn't sure how much longer she could continue to live like this. Bedtime she made sure she was asleep before he climbed in, because she was afraid he would reject her affection if she asked him to make love to her. Bianca didn't know why she was beating herself up about it. They had an agreement and London was sticking to his end of the deal. She just hoped that, in time, things would get back to the way they were and eventually he would find it in his heart to truly love her.

Bianca dried off, then moved over to the full-length mirror behind the door, taking a good look at her tummy sideways. It was no longer flat. At five months' pregnant, her belly had begun to protrude. She realized it yesterday when her favorite jeans no longer fit.

She, Danica and Brenna were going shopping over the weekend for maternity clothes. She noticed that her breasts had also grown, preparing for the baby. New bras were in order, as well. Bianca wrinkled her nose at her reflection. She could no longer get around it. She officially looked pregnant.

Before leaving the bathroom, she stepped on a scale in the corner and gasped. She had gained eight pounds.

Suddenly, she burst into tears. She moved into the bedroom, slipped on an oversize T-shirt and shorts and crawled onto the bed. Before long she was going to be as big as a minivan!

London tapped lightly on their bedroom door and waited. When there was no answer, he peeked inside. "Bianca, are you okay? Bianca?"

She bolted upright at the sound of his voice and wiped her eyes with the balls of her hands. London stood just inside the door, wearing a worried look. "I'm fine," she answered.

Pushing away from the door, he took a closer look. "Have you been crying?"

Bianca leapt to her feet. "Look at me, London," she said, pulling her shirt up so he could see her growing belly. "I've gained eight pounds!" She gave him a side view. "Before long I'm going to look like a whale."

He nodded. Actually, she looked downright adorable, but he knew he'd never convince her. "I wouldn't count on wearing a bikini any time soon," he said instead, with a wink.

Bianca reached for her pillow and threw it at him. He ducked. "Hey, I was just kidding," he said, laughing. "And stop crying. It's just your hormones."

She looked at him. "How do you know?"

"Because it's what women go through. You're body is going

through a lot of changes right now. When is your next doctor's appointment?"

"Next week."

London walked over to the side of the bed and took a seat. "You need to talk to him. Matter of fact, talk to Brenna. She's on her third child. If anyone should know about mood swings, it's her."

Bianca briefly dropped her eyes and giggled. "You're right about that."

London dropped his gaze, admiring how much her body had changed in such a short period. Her breasts were fuller and her stomach round. And he thought she looked sexier than ever.

"You want to go with me to Dairy Queen?"

"I'm in my pajamas."

"We'll order at the drive-through window. Nobody will see you."

"I'll go, but all I'm getting is a small ice cream cone. I need to start dieting and watching my weight. No more lasagna for me." She grabbed a pair of flip-flops from under the bed. London picked up his keys and they headed out to his SUV.

He unlocked her door and opened it. Once he joined her in the front seat, he found her looking at him strangely. "What?"

"You think I'm fat, don't you?"

"No, I don't think you're fat."

Turning on her seat, she looked dead at him. "Then why are you taking me out for ice cream?"

"Because you made dinner and I thought some ice cream would be nice to cheer you up."

"Oh" was all she said, then settled on the seat and stared out the window.

He pulled into Dairy Queen and stopped at the drive-through window. Bianca ordered an ice cream sundae and London ordered a chocolate-dipped cone. When they pulled away a few minutes later, London couldn't help but shoot side glances at her.

She stopped licking her spoon. "What?"

"You've sort of blown your diet, haven't you?"

She blushed as she looked at the size of the large cup of carbs and calories she's ordered. "I'm starting tomorrow."

Once they arrived home and had settled on the couch, he

gazed down at her watching the way she licked the spoon, imagining her tongue licking something else. Feeling his body growing hard, he cleared his throat. "I'll got some figures to work up. I'll be in my office if you need anything." He turned and didn't dare look back; otherwise, he'd have taken her right then and there in the living room.

If he had turned around, he would have seen the look of disappointment on Bianca's face.

Chapter 27

Two weeks after their trip to Dairy Queen, Bianca left work early for an appointment with her obstetrician. Dr. Lampton was a handsome and happily married physician who had delivered both her nieces and her nephew. Sheyna had recommended him, and immediately she felt at ease with him. After his physical examination, he asked her to meet him in his office. She had just taken the seat across from him when his nurse stepped into the room. "Dr. Lampton, sorry to interrupt, but Bianca, your husband is here. May I bring him back?"

Bianca was sure she had the wrong room. "My husband?" she managed to say. When the nurse nodded, she shrugged her shoulders and was sure she looked totally confused. "Sure, uh, send him on back." When the nurse left, Bianca was convinced that she was going to realize her mistake and come back to apologize for the mixup.

A moment later London stepped inside the office. "Sorry I'm late," he said silkily when he reached her, then leaned over and dropped a kissed on her mouth, which was hanging wide open. He introduced himself to Dr. Lampton and they shook hands.

"It is such a pleasure to meet you. I like to meet all the fathers before the birth of their babies if I can. Congratulations to the two of you on your first child. Hopefully, the Lord will bless you with many more," the doctor said to London. "Mr. Brown, your wife is at twenty-one weeks. The baby is developing right on schedule."

London reached over and squeezed her hand. "That's good news."

Dr. Lampton cupped his hands on his desk. "Do either of you have any questions for me?"

Bianca shook her head. London looked over at her, then back at the obstetrician and cleared his throat. "Actually, Dr. Lampton I have a question."

"Sure."

"How long is it okay for us to…" He purposely allowed his voice to trail off. From one man to another, Dr. Lampton knew what he was getting at. Bianca felt her nipples pucker.

"You and Bianca can have sex during the pregnancy as long as she feels comfortable. Bianca knows that if she experiences any abdominal pain or bleeding she needs to call me immediately."

London met her eyes and she did not miss the desire burning in their depths.

Dr. Lampton turned to Bianca. "Well, if you don't have any other questions, young lady, I'll see you next month. Mr. Brown, it was a pleasure."

They rose and left his office. With his hand at the small of her back, London steered them down the long hall. Bianca didn't say anything until they were outside. "How did you know I was here?" she asked.

London stopped walking, and turned and faced her. "I saw it on the calendar." He frowned. "Why didn't you ask me to come with you?"

After several moments of intense silence, she replied, "London, I didn't think you wanted to come."

"Well, I do." Standing in front of her, he raised his hand and rested it on her round belly. "Remember, that's my child you're carrying. Besides, I care about you and I promise to be there every step of the way."

Because he promised to be there. She wished he was here because he loved her and this was where he wanted to be.

"Thank you."

"You're welcome," he said and focused his attention on her mouth. Doing so caused her breathing to quicken. Her lips began to tingle. Deciding that a kiss was the only cure for her beating heartbeat, she leaned forward and tilted her face toward him.

London didn't need any further hints. A moan surged from his throat the moment his lips pressed down on hers. Instantly, she opened to him, inviting the mating of his tongue. Desire beat in her blood and drummed in her ears, consuming her mind and heart. Need radiated from him, as well. She felt it in the intensity of their kiss. She felt it as their bodies came together, making her aware that he was hard and aroused.

Breaking off the kiss, he looked down at her and she saw the hunger in his eyes. His gaze was intense, determined. "What do you have scheduled for the rest of the afternoon?"

Bianca had felt that kiss clear down to her toes. Sexual tension surrounded them. She tried to slow her breath and slow her pulse, but nothing could bring calmness to her body, which was tense with wanting him. "Nothing," she said, after inhaling deeply and blowing out a rush of air. "I was planning to spend the rest of the afternoon at home."

"Good, because I plan to spend the rest of the day with my wife." London curled his fingers around hers and escorted Bianca to her car, then helped her in and kissed her again before walking away.

"Oh, boy. I'm in deep trouble," she said to herself as she started her car and followed her husband home.

That evening, London insisted on taking Bianca out to dinner. Over the last two weeks, the morning sickness had ceased and her appetite had increased—considerably. He watched with amusement as she finished a KC strip steak, a loaded potato and asparagus and then asked for the dessert menu. They shared a slice of Granny Smith apple pie with vanilla ice cream, then headed home.

As soon as they stepped into their bedroom, he pulled her into his arms. Slowly, he undressed his wife, guided her over to the bed then planted kisses in every area imaginable. He caressed the roundness of her belly, then moved his mouth to nuzzle her there.

She whispered his name as he moved even lower. When he couldn't wait a second longer, Bianca nestled him between her parted thighs, ready and eager for him to become one with her. He felt more than physical lust for the woman who gazed up at him with sparkling eyes. His feeling for Bianca was love. London brought his mouth to hers as he entered her.

Slowly, he began to move. There was no need to rush. As far as he was concerned, they had the rest of their lives. Heat began to build and Bianca raised her hips and met his thrusts, and it wasn't long before she was crying out his name and he hers shortly afterward.

Rolling over, he pulled her into his arms and held her tightly as their heart rates slowed.

"I've missed holding and touching you," he confessed.

"Me, too," she admitted and he could tell by her heavy sigh that the admission had been difficult for her.

"Then we will have to make sure that we continue to find time for each other."

He held her, but could tell that she hadn't fallen asleep. "What are you thinking about?"

She gave a frustrated sigh. "London, I'm scared about us. I'm scared because I'm five months' pregnant and I don't know the first thing about being a mother."

He chuckled softly and dropped a kiss on the top of her head, his hold on her tightening. "You're going to make a wonderful mother, Bianca, so stop worrying."

Her cheek was against his chest. She was sure to hear the strong beat of his heart. "I can't help it. I've never done this before."

"Neither have I, but we're going to do fine. Bianca you are the most caring woman I know. I've seen you with your niece. You're going to be a fabulous mother."

"And you're going to be a wonderful father."

"Thanks, because I'm scared to death," he said and the two of them laughed like a long-married couple.

"As for us. Don't worry. I've never cared about a woman they way I care about you. So much has happened these last several weeks that I need to ask something of you."

"Okay."

"Forget about the agreement. Forget about the father of your baby. All I want you to do is focus on the three of us, your husband, our baby and you, and the life we can have together. I want you to allow whatever happens to happen and when the time comes we can evaluate our relationship and decide at that time how we want to spend the rest of our lives. How does that sound to you?"

She was silent for so long he thought she had fallen asleep.

"Bianca?"

She raised herself up and he saw the tears that brimmed her eyes and the smile on her lips. His heart skipped a beat. *Did that mean she had feelings for him, too?* he wondered.

"I think that sounds like a wonderful idea." She then kissed him. London groaned then rolled her onto her back.

They were going to be just fine, and he was going to enjoy it for as long as she allowed him in her life. As far as he was concerned, the end would never come.

Chapter 28

She went to work the next day with a smile on her face. There was no point in denying it. She knew with all her heart that she wanted her marriage to work. She wanted it to last longer than the twelve months and, after what London said, she had a feeling he wanted the same thing. And that was fine with her. No more holding back. She was going to show London just how much she loved him.

Around four, Bianca decided to leave work early. She had been trying to improve her cooking skills and decided to try her hand at fried chicken. Grabbing her briefcase, she headed out of the office and waved goodbye to her staff as she approached the elevator. After exiting the building, she walked across the parking lot, when someone jumped in front of her and caused her to start.

"Hey, baby," he smiled. "I've missed you."

Bianca was flabbergasted to see Collin standing right in front of her. It had been weeks since he'd shown up in her town house, yet he had the nerve to pop up as if it had just been yesterday. She swallowed hard and tried to keep her anger at bay.

She studied Collin's face. His nose was too thin, his forehead wide and his chin weak, not strong and square, like London's. She wondered what she had ever seen in him.

Collin leaned back against the hood of her car. Bianca silently groaned and cursed herself for leaving early. If she had stayed a few minutes longer, he would have entered the hotel and she could have had security escort him out. Hungry and eager to get home, she pursed her lips. "Collin, what do you want?"

"You. I want you back."

Bianca was speechless for a moment. *How could he just waltz over here and think she would take him back after the way he had treated her?* she wondered. She felt furious, hurt and a surge of other emotions all at once.

"Collin, go away," she hissed then reached for her key and walked over to the driver's side.

He stood up straight. "Your marriage may have fooled everybody, but it didn't fool me."

Her stomach churned. "What is that supposed to mean?"

"That's my baby you're carrying." He pointed to her stomach. Her pregnancy was obvious in the pleated blue maternity top. "And you're not keeping me from it. I'll get a DNA test. Then I'm going to sue you for joint custody. No court will keep me away from what's mine."

"Whatever," she said and tried not be appear affected by his threats when, in reality, she was shaking in her heels.

Collin laughed long and hard. "Just think, when that baby spends summers with me, you're going to have to pay me child support. Now won't that be something."

Anger stiffened her spine. She was ready to give him a piece of her mind, but she didn't want to let him know how much he'd upset her.

"Really?" she snapped irritably. "Well, we'll see about that. No court would give a two-timer like you a child."

"We'll just have to see."

"We will." She had a baby to protect. "London is the father of my child."

"We'll see about that, Bianca. I devoted six months of my life to you. That has to be worth something. And remember this—if you won't share custody, I'll sue for full custody. You'll hear from my lawyers."

Her blood ran cold. "And you'll hear from mine if you keep harassing me."

He turned on his heels and walked to the other end of the parking lot, whistling merrily.

Bianca raced over and emptied her stomach behind a shrub. When the sickness relented, she stumbled to her car and stabbed the key in the ignition with a trembling hand. She had to get home. She placed her hands on her belly and whispered, "That man will never get his hands on you, my darling. Not if I have anything to do with it." By the time she reached home she had it set in her mind that she was going to do whatever it took to keep him away from her child.

Chapter 29

The following afternoon, her lawyer's words made the bottom fall out of her stomach.

If Collin insisted on a paternity test and the test proved he was the father of the child, he did have rights. The lawyer's advice was that they work out some kind of visitation agreement.

Bianca slammed down the phone. The last thing she wanted was to share her child with someone like Collin Clark. *How in the world had she ever thought she was in love with him?*

She leaned back in her chair and placed a protective hand on her stomach. She wasn't going to share her baby with him. The only man she wanted to be the father of her child was her husband. London.

She felt the baby move and a smile curled her lips. Her baby knew who her daddy was. London had taken her yesterday to shop for nursery furniture. As they looked at cribs, a couple of residents of Sheraton Beach stopped to congratulate them. The pride on London's face was priceless. The rest of the evening was spent lying on the couch together trying to come up with baby names.

All Collin cared about was the money. After giving it further thought, she picked up the phone and called him on his cell phone.

He answered with a chuckle. "I see you've finally come to your senses."

"Let's meet tomorrow and talk."

"I'd be delighted to."

He was still laughing as she hung up.

Chapter 30

Diamere signed on all the spots indicated on the contract, then handed it across the table with a big grin. "Man, it's definitely great doing business with you."

"Absolutely," London said as he took the contract, folded it and put it in his breast pocket.

"Now just keep making us money."

"Most definitely," London replied with confidence.

Diamere had kept a twenty percent interest in the restaurant. The prime location with the correct management was going to be a gold mine.

London reached for his burger with a smile on his lips. "Bianca said you bought a couple of nightclubs."

"Yep. Nice, classy spots. The price was too good to pass up. The owner went to prison for real estate fraud and the family was desperate to sell to cover his legal expenses," Diamere said between bites. "I've been waiting three years for this day to come. My clubs are gonna be off the hook."

"I'll have to drive up and check them out." London bit into his burger and he and Diamere talked while they ate. The food wasn't bad, he had to admit. Diamere had suggested meeting at the Beaumont Hotel, since he had driven down for the night. London was more than happy to meet him and share lunch because afterwards he planned to stop by the hotel flower shop and pick up two dozen roses for his wife before going to her office and surprising her. The plan was to convince her to play hooky for the rest of the afternoon and spend the next several hours at home wrapped in his arms.

"So, can I ask, how's married life?" Diamere asked, breaking into London's thoughts. He'd been so busy planning the rest of the afternoon, he had honestly forgotten that Diamere was still sitting across from him.

"Good... Bianca definitely makes me happy."

Diamere grinned and looked pleased. "I'm happy for the both of you, really I am. Aunt Jessica should be quite pleased she's gotten all her children married off. Jabarie and Brenna are expecting baby number three, Jace and Sheyna have a little boy, Jaden and Danica's baby is right around the corner and now Bianca's expecting. Aunt Jessica is going to have plenty of little ones running around that big old house of hers. I would pay a thousand bucks to see one of them break something."

While chewing on a fry, London chuckled. His mother-in-law could be a little high strung at times, but she was a totally different woman with her grandchildren.

"What about you? When are you going to settle down and start a family?"

Diamere scowled. "Nah, not me. Last time I tried that I got burned—badly." While they finished eating, Diamere told London about his girlfriend claiming to be pregnant with his twins. He married her only to find out the babies weren't his. Instead, they belonged to a married man she was still involved with.

"Man, shit happens. Don't give up. There's someone out there for everyone."

Diamere gave him a long, hard stare. "There was someone. A schoolteacher named Kelly. Kelly Saunders. But I broke it off when Rachel told me she was pregnant. Last I heard, Kelly was married and living in Texas."

He reached for his beer. "The only women I need now is my

nightclubs—Ja'net, Diamond and Hadley." They chuckled then finished their food and said their goodbyes. London made plans to stop by the restaurant in a week, so he could meet the staff and start transitioning things.

While Diamere, who insisted on paying the bill, waited for his change, London headed across the marble floor of the lobby to the flower shop. He placed the order and while the clerk put together a beautiful arrangement, he pushed his hands in his pocket and stared off toward the fountain at the center of lobby.

He noticed Bianca standing near the revolving door with her hand pressed against her stomach. He felt the feeling in his gut. In less than four months a little Brown would be coming into the world.

He was tempted to walk across the lobby and scoop her up in his arms, but it would ruin the surprise. Hopefully, Bianca wouldn't run into Diamere on his way back up to his room.

"Would you like me to add a little baby's breath?"

He tore his eyes away from his beautiful wife long enough to say, "Yes, that would be great, and one single white rose."

"Ooooh! Mr. Brown you are so romantic. Ms. Bianca is lucky to have you."

He noticed the envy in the woman's face before she went back to work.

No. I'm the lucky one, he thought as he returned his attention to Bianca and watched the direction of her eyes as a man who looked familiar came toward her.

As soon as he grinned, London recognized him—Collin.

What the hell was he doing here?

He moved forward ready, to confront the dude and froze in his tracks when Collin strolled up beside Bianca and pressed his lips to her cheek. She rewarded him with a smile, then they walked to the front desk with his hand resting comfortably on the small of her back.

London stood there, clenching his fist while he watched. The desk clerk handed Collin a key and he and Bianca headed past the corporation elevators to the set at the far left that led to the twenty-three floors of guestrooms.

Bianca leaned in and whispered something close to Collin's

ear that made him smile. London stood and watched as the two of them boarded the elevator with the door closing behind them.

London was stunned beyond words. His wife was having an affair with her baby's daddy.

Chapter 31

Bianca waited until they were inside the penthouse suite before she reared back and slapped Collin hard across the face. "Don't you ever put your mouth on me again!"

He chuckled as he raised a hand to his cheek. "My bad. I thought maybe I'd have one for old times' sake."

"We have no 'old times' to reminisce about."

She was so angry that it took everything she had to contain herself while they were in the lobby. To keep her staff from over-hearing, she had whispered close to his ear that he was a creep.

"Wow!" he began as he moved around the room, taking in the rich-grain woods and fine upscale furnishings in royal blue and beige. "This is really nice. I knew your hotels were fabulous, but I didn't think they were this fine." A look of smug self-satisfaction crossed his face. "I feel like I stepped into royalty." He flopped down onto the couch and spread his arms along the tops of the cushions. Grinning like a man with a secret.

She rolled her eyes.

Folding his arms across his chest, he turned his head and faced her. "You said you wanted to talk. So let's talk."

"I want to know what it's going to take for you to get out of my life once and for all."

He chuckled and the sound was starting to grate on her nerves. "Bianca, I don't see that happening for at least the next eighteen years. That's my baby you're carrying."

"Listen, I am married to London and he is ready to adopt this baby and raise her or him as his own."

He gave her a long look. "I thought you knew me better than that. There is no way I would give up the rights of my child."

"Why not? You've got another woman."

"Yes, but that doesn't have anything to do with my unborn child." His lips curled upward. "Face it, Bianca, I'm going to be around for a long time."

She glared over at him. "I'll get a lawyer and fight you."

"Go for it. Any good lawyer will tell you that you can't deny me my parental rights."

"Then it will be a long fight."

"Sure, and in the meantime I'll let the whole world know I am the real father of your child. You know how much you hate scandal. Mommie Dearest will have a fit."

Bastard. He was determined to blackmail her.

"By the way, thanks for the room. I'll be needing it until Sunday. I'm sure Daddy won't mind me charging everything to my room." He rose, strolled over to the bar, removed a bottle of liquor and popped it open.

There was a long pause before Bianca reached into her purse and removed her checkbook. "Okay, Collin. How much is this going to cost me?"

His lips curled upward. "Now that's more like it."

Chapter 32

Bianca returned home well after six o'clock. After Collin had laughed in her face at her offer, she left the hotel and drove around for a couple of hours, trying to decide what to do next. Collin was going to cause her a lot of trouble if she didn't let him see the baby.

She pulled the car into the garage beside London's SUV and released a heavy sigh. He was home early today. Bianca turned off the car and sat there for the longest time, trying to decide what to do next. *Should I tell my husband?* she wondered.

After weighing the pros and cons, Bianca decided it wasn't a good idea to mention Collin's demands just yet, until she knew for sure how she was going to handle the situation. There had to be a way to put this to rest. Collin was the baby's father, and as far as her lawyer was concerned, he had a right to be a part of her unborn child's life.

She moved inside the house through the laundry room, removed her heels and left them beside the door. She then padded inside the kitchen and stopped in her tracks.

"Hey, baby."

London removed a casserole dish from the oven, placed it on the stove then swung around. "Hey, you're late," he said, then studied her intensely with his eyes.

"Yes, I had a late meeting this afternoon," she mumbled, quickly moving across the tile floor and kissing her husband on his cheek. "I see that you cooked."

"I figured you'd probably be hungry."

"I am, sweetheart." She gave him another kiss then released him. "Let me go and change, and I'll be right back."

When she came back, she was dressed in stretch pants and a comfortable T-shirt. She stepped into the kitchen. London had already set the kitchen table.

"Mmm, that looks good," she said and took a seat. "How did everything go with my cousin?"

"Great. I'll be meeting with him again next week."

She smiled. "Excellent."

As they ate, they discussed the plans they had for the restaurant. Afterwards, they moved into the living room. It wasn't until then that she realized how distant and distracted London seemed.

"Sweetheart, is something wrong?"

"I've been thinking, and I think this is a mistake."

"What's a mistake?"

London's eyes grew cold as he looked at her on the other end of the couch. "Us, going into business together. Creating this family image."

Her stomach began to turn. "What brought this on?"

He rose and paced the length of the room. "I've been thinking," he said. "We need to remember that our marriage is a temporary business arrangement and nothing more. We have less than a year left together and we need to remember that at that point we'll be going separate ways. I think we need to keep reminding ourselves that our marriage isn't real."

Her heart sank. "That's not what you said the other day."

A hard, furious look came into his eyes. "Can't a man change his mind?"

She swallowed. "I see."

"I think it's better this way." London rose and headed out of the room, then stopped but didn't bother to turn around. "I'm going out. Don't wait up."

He went to his room. A few moments later she heard the garage door open, and he pulled out of the driveway and was gone.

Chapter 33

London held up his empty glass and signaled for the barmaid to bring him another rum and coke. She nodded her head in acknowledgment, then reached inside the cooler, retrieved a bottle of beer and lowered it on the counter in front of a customer at the other end of the bar.

While he waited, he allowed his gaze to travel around Spanky's, a sports bar that was the happening place on a Wednesday night in Sheraton Beach. A professional basketball game was playing on the big screen, and the Lakers were leading by seven points, but the playoffs were the last thing on his mind. No matter how much he tried to push it aside, he could not seem to get Bianca and Collin out of his mind.

Every emotion he could think of was running through his heart. Anger, jealousy and love led the race. As far as he was concerned, Bianca was his wife and the child she was carrying was his.

A fresh drink was put on the bar in front of him. He thanked the barmaid, then tossed it back, finishing it in two swallows.

"Give me another," he ordered as he slammed the glass on the counter.

The barmaid turned around and gave him a concerned look. "Sexy, I think you need to slow down."

London gave her a dismissive wave. He'd been running a tab for the last two hours, and now she wanted to start complaining. "Sandy, quit acting like my mother and give me another one."

Mumbling under her breath, she resumed pouring the contents of a shaker into a martini glass, then garnished it with an apple slice. "London, why don't you go on home to that beautiful little wife of yours."

He responded to her suggestion with pursed lips and a single raised brow that caused her lips to form in an *O*. The message came across loud and clear. There was trouble in paradise. Sandy nodded and moved to the other end of the bar.

Staring straight in front of him, London caught his reflection in the mirror behind the bar. What he saw caused him to rake a hand down the length of his face. Pathetic.

What right do you have to be jealous? he wondered. Bianca had made it clear from day one that their marriage would be one of convenience only. The sex was just a bonus. In no way was love now or ever supposed to have come into play. They agreed to stay together for one year and part without scandal as friends.

So what's the problem?

The problem was that somewhere along the way his emotions had gotten involved and he had fallen in love with his wife. After their honeymoon and with her agreeing to let whatever happened happen, he thought that maybe, just maybe, Bianca had fallen in love with him, too.

Sucker.

London scowled at the man in the mirror for being so stupid and for letting his guard down.

The crowd yelled, drawing his attention to the television. Apparently, Kobe Bryant hit a three-pointer, giving the Lakers a twelve-point lead. *At least someone was having a good night,* he thought.

Sandy returned with a drink and a firm warning that it would be his last. London thanked her for the drink, then moved over to a table in the corner and took a seat. In an attempt to push thoughts of Bianca aside, he managed to watch bits and pieces of the next quarter of the game. After a while his body as well as his mind had relaxed. The liquor had finally begun to kick in. Good.

"I hear you need a ride."

He looked up to see Jaden standing over him. "Don't know where you got that crazy idea from." But even as he asked, with a side glance he spotted Sandy glancing in their direction. She had seen the two of them in there often enough to know who to call to pick him up.

"Have a seat and a beer."

"Nah, one of us needs to drive." Jaden straddled the chair across from him, then leaned forward, resting his elbows on the table.

"Shouldn't you be at home with your wife?" London snapped, his eyes blazing over at Jaden.

Jaden frowned and reached for a handful of popcorn on the table. "She's at one of those home-decorating parties."

London nodded, then turned his attention to the game. Jaden swung his chair around and followed suit.

"I need to say something before the game comes back on," Jaden said during a commercial break. He glanced down at his hands and up again. "I owe you a big apology."

London reached for his glass and took a sip. "About what?"

"Collin. Bianca told me everything."

Surprise flickered through London's brown eyes. "So you know—"

"I know you married her to save the family from scandal. I know that you're not the father—"

"I *am* the father. That little boy is mine."

Jaden grinned. "Good answer."

London lowered his glass while Jaden continued.

"I'll admit I wasn't too happy to know my best friend was messing with my sister behind my back, but after seeing how happy she is and after her telling me how much she loves you, I've changed my mind. You have my blessing, man."

Jaden continued to talk but all London heard was *how much she loves you*. "Bianca told you she loves me?"

Jaden shrugged. "Yeah, not that she needed to. It was written all over her face."

Why hadn't she ever bothered to tell him? Probably the same reason why he'd never told her. Too damn stubborn.

But if she loved me why was she with Collin? "Look I got to go." Without explanation, he rose from the chair and hurried across the bar. Jaden came right behind him.

"Whoa! Hold on there. You're not going anywhere," Jaden said, as he grabbed London's arm.

London looked down at his hand then back at Jaden. "I need to get home and nothing is going to stop me from getting there."

"That's why I'm here."

"Then take me home now," London demanded.

As far as London was concerned, Jaden didn't drive fast enough. Before he even had the car parked, London jumped out and raced into the house. He wasn't in there five minutes when it hit him. Bianca had left him.

He walked the length of the house one more time. This had to be some kind of mistake. As he made his way down the hall a third time, Jaden grabbed his arm.

"London, man, she's not here."

"Where is she?"

Jaden shrugged. "I'm not sure, but it can't be too hard to figure out. Not in this little town. Let me make a few phone calls."

London raked a hand across his head as he moved back to the bedroom to check for a note or something. Two minutes later he lowered himself onto the bed. Nothing.

His wife was gone and it was all his fault.

She loves you.

Then where was she? he wondered. Jealousy started to rear its little head again. Maybe she was with Collin. Visions formed in his head of her lying in her lover's arms.

He heard footsteps coming down the hall. He looked up to find Jaden standing in the door. "Bianca's at my parents' house."

He rose from the bed. "Then let's go and get her."

"Oh, no! You need to get some sleep and sober up a bit. You can talk to her tomorrow." Jaden pushed him back down onto the bed.

"She left me, didn't she?" he searched his brother-in-law's eyes for answers.

Jaden hesitated. "Mother said Bianca was very upset. She asked to stay in her old room for a few days. It's probably for the best."

London pulled his keys out of his pocket and tried getting up again. "I have to talk to her."

"Not tonight. It is too late to be knocking at Mother's door unless you want to get on her bad side. Trust me, man, you don't want to piss my mother off."

He was quiet for a long moment before he nodded.

Jaden snatched his keys from his hand. "I'll keep these and bring them back in the morning on my way to work. Get some rest." He headed toward the door.

"Jaden?" London called after him.

He looked over his shoulder. "Yeah?"

"I love her."

Jaden's shoulders sagged as he nodded. "I believe you. That's how I know the two of you will be okay."

London watched him leave, hoping he was right.

Chapter 34

"Bianca, sweetie. You know I love you, but you can't stay with me forever."

Bianca looked over at her so-called best friend and rolled her eyes. "Some friend you are." Actually, Debra had been a wonderful friend, allowing Bianca to crash at her house after her mother started getting on her nerves. She could have easily taken a suite at the hotel but then she'd have to run the risk of bumping into that snake Collin, who was still there milking the hotel for everything he could.

"Because I'm your friend and because I love you, I'm going to tell you like it is." Debra paused and scowled. "Go home and work out your marriage."

"According to my husband, I don't have a marriage. I have an arrangement. Believe me. London has already said more than enough." Bianca felt sick to her stomach every time she thought about their last conversation.

Debra took a seat on the rose-upholstered couch, shaking her head with disbelief. "I still can't believe London said that. Are you sure you heard him right?"

"Yes, I heard him right. Goodness, Debra, whose side are you on?"

"Yours, of course, but I'm trying to be open-minded."

"And so am I. But it is what it is. If London doesn't think our arrangement is working out, what else is there to say?"

"That you love him. And you want your marriage to work."

Bianca frowned at that idea. "There is no way in hell I'm putting myself out there like that for him to throw my words back in my face. I love him, but there is no way I'm going to beg him to be with me or my child." She leaned back on the armchair and blew out a big breath. "I've got enough problems right now dealing with Collin."

Debra gave a rude snort. "That isn't even worth wasting your breath on. Tell that man to go to hell and kick him out on his butt."

"Right, and he'll drag me to court so fast my head will spin."

"So let him. What's the worst that can happen?"

She bored angry eyes in Debra's direction. "Him getting joint custody of my child. Collin has no interest whatsoever in having children. The only reason he's interested now is because of my money."

Debra leaned forward with her elbows resting on her knees. "I told you that man was scum."

"Yes, I know, but this is not the time for I told you so. I've got big problems. No husband and a father I need to pay to stay away from my child."

Debra shook her head with disbelief. "Are you seriously going to give him money?"

Dragging a leg to her chin, she gave a reluctant nod. "Yep. Whatever it takes. I'm meeting him at the bar in the hotel tomorrow evening with a check."

"You know it's never going to stop. As soon as the money runs out, he'll be back at your door demanding more." Debra pursed her lips with disgust.

"No. I'm not that stupid. I had my lawyer draw up papers for him to sign. The second he cashes that check, he'll relinquish all rights to his child."

Grinning, Debra mumbled, "I guess you're smarter than you look."

Bianca snorted rudely. "Not smart enough obviously, otherwise, I'd know what to do to get my husband to love me."

It was well after seven o'clock and London was in his office at the back of the restaurant, going over the supply orders. He'd been looking at the same thing and still couldn't seem to get the ordering right. All he could do was think about his wife.

London tried for over a week. Making phone calls, arriving at Beaumont Manor unannounced, but nothing worked. Bianca refused to talk to him. Then yesterday Jaden told him that Bianca was no longer staying at his parents'. Unfortunately, he had no idea where she was staying. London spent the entire evening wondering if she was now living with Collin.

He reached for an eraser, removed an entry that he'd added twice, tried to brush Bianca from his mind and told himself that it was probably for the best. She and Collin and the baby could now live happily ever after.

At that thought, the pencil he'd been holding snapped in half. That was his child she was carrying and Bianca was his wife! The question was what was he going to do to get them back?

"Knock knock."

His eyes snapped in the direction of the door, where he found Debra boring angry eyes at him. "What's wrong?"

"What's wrong is your marriage," she began with her hands at her hips. "I came over here to see what you're planning to do about it."

"Nothing."

"Nothing? London, I'm surprised at you. I really thought you loved Bianca."

"I do. My wife doesn't love me."

She chuckled. "Then you're blind. That woman is so crazy about you that that is all I heard last night and this morning."

His brow rose. "Bianca's staying with you?"

Debra frowned. "Where else would she be staying?"

He looked over at her, then finally shrugged his broad shoulders. "I figured—"

Her eyes narrowed suspiciously. "You figured what?"

There was no point in beating around the bush. It wasn't as

if it were a secret. "I figured she and Collin were trying to work things out."

"Work things out? Puhleeze," she said with a rude snort. "The only thing that creep wants is money."

"Money?"

She moved into the chair across from his desk and told him about Collin blackmailing Bianca for money. The more she talked, the angrier he got.

It had all been a big misunderstanding. He had put the brakes on his relationship and hurt his wife's feelings all for nothing.

"She's meeting that creep tomorrow night."

"Not if I can help it." Abruptly, he rose from the chair and reached for his keys. He was going to get his wife back, but first he needed to deal with Collin.

Chapter 35

The following afternoon London knocked heavily on the double doors to the penthouse suite. It wasn't long before he heard heavy footsteps across the carpet and the door opened.

"Yeah?"

London looked at the man standing on the other side of the door and forced a tight smile. "Collin Clark?"

"Who's asking…" His voice trailed off as a lightbulb went off in his head. "Hey, don't I know you?"

"No, but you're about to." Without waiting for an invitation, London pushed past him and stepped into the spacious room. Plush, cream carpet. Blue furnishings. A fully stocked bar in the corner. According to the hotel staff, Collin had been greedily helping himself to the bar. In fact, the hotel bill had already reached five figures.

"Hey, wait a minute. I didn't invite you in."

London swung around and glared at the shorter man, who quickly pulled back, realizing that he was no match for London Brown. "I'm here on my wife's behalf."

"You're Bianca's husband?"

"Yes." And nothing or no one was going to change that.

Collin's lips curled upward and he rubbed his palms together eagerly. "Well, good. I guess she sent you over with the check. Sorry, buddy, but if you're going to be raising that little crumb snatcher as yours, it's going to cost you."

It took everything London had not to punch him in the face right then and there. Instead, London chuckled and moved over to the bar and helped himself to a small bottle of Hennessy.

"What's so funny?"

"You. If you think my wife and I are going to pay you one cent."

He glared over at him. "If she doesn't, I'll tell everyone I am the father of her child and the last thing she wants is a long, drawn-out custody battle."

"Actually, we're looking forward to it."

"What?"

"Sure. Just make sure you invite your wife, Kathy."

"My wife?"

"I'm sorry… I meant *wives*. We need to tell Charlene, as well."

Collin grew still.

London set down his drink, then reached inside his breast pocket and pulled out a small manila envelope and tossed it on the counter. "I've been doing some checking on you. Go ahead—take a look."

With hesitation, Collin moved over to the counter and looked inside the envelope.

"You'll find your marriage certificate to Kathy and one to Charlene just last year. She was the pretty woman I spotted you with in Chester. After I went and talked to your chief master sergeant, I discovered that the military was only aware of your marriage to Kathy."

Collin swore and his face turned a shade paler.

"Bigamy is a violation of the Uniform Code of Military Justice and punishable by law."

"Well, I…" He couldn't find the words.

London came around the counter, then took Collin by the collar and slammed him against the wall. "You made a big mistake when you tried to mess with my family. That's my wife and child. If you ever go near either one of them again, I'll personally make sure you never see another day."

"I'm sorry. I'll leave town tomorrow."

"No, you're leaving this afternoon." London shoved him once more, then released him. He removed a document from the envelope, then reached inside his pocket. Collin ducked and shielded his head before he realized that London was holding a pen.

"Here, I need you to sign these papers, giving up your parental rights."

Collin didn't bat an eye as he reached for the legal document on the counter and signed and dated every spot indicated with an *X*. As soon as he was done, London folded up the document, stuck it in his pocket and walked out the door without uttering another word. As soon as he was at the end of the hall, London nodded at the two men standing there waiting and said, "He's all yours." As he pushed the down arrow for the elevator, he watched the military police walk into the suite and arrest Collin.

Collin would never mess with his family again. Now it was up to him to get them back.

Chapter 36

London rang Debra's doorbell. He wasn't sure how Bianca was going to react when she saw him, but it was a chance he had to take.

Bianca opened the door, realized it was him and pursed her lips. "What do you want?" she asked, gripping the doorknob tightly.

"You. I want you. Please tell me that we still have a chance."

Ignoring him, she turned on her heels and walked into the living room. London followed and stood in the doorway as she returned to the couch, curling her legs underneath her, and resumed watching a television program.

London moved closer, feeling just an inkling of hope. She hadn't slammed the door in his face, so that had to be a good sign.

"Bianca, listen to me. I was wrong. I saw you in the hotel lobby with Collin and jumped to conclusions."

She turned, her eyes wide with surprise. "You thought I wanted Collin back?" When he nodded, she turned her head, clearly disappointed.

"I know. I was wrong." He saw tears in the corner of her eyes and it nearly killed him. "I want you back home with me. I miss you."

"Why do you miss me? Like you said, it was only a business arrangement, so what difference would it make to you if I was there or not? Obviously, if it was that easy to say that our relationship was a mistake I couldn't have meant that much to you."

"You are important. Very important." He walked over to the couch and dropped down on one knee in front of her.

"In the time that we've been together, I realized I can't live without you."

She shook her head. "And when did you come to this realization?"

"When I no longer had you in my life."

She dragged her legs up to her chest and rested her chin on top of her knees. "I don't think it's going to work out between us. That whole arrangement stuff was kind of stupid."

"I don't want you to be with me because of the arrangement. I want you to want me for me. And to make sure there is nothing standing between us, you don't have to worry about Collin ever again." London reached inside his pocket, pulled out the legal document, then told her everything that he had found out about Collin, the bigamist.

The look on her face was a combination of anger and relief.

"So we don't have to stay married a year." It was a statement not a question.

London shook his head. "No, we don't have to. But I want to." He took hold of her shoulders, pulled her close to him and looked into her eyes. "I want you—and not for just a year. I want you for a lifetime."

"London," she began, as a single tear ran down her cheek. "I don't know…"

"Sweetheart. It can work between us. I know it can. I want a real marriage. I have fallen in love with my wife. Please come home with me."

The room began to spin as Bianca stared at her husband, down on the floor begging her to come home with him. His chest was heaving and fear was in his eyes. He was so handsome and he had just confessed that he was in love with her.

She tilted her head slightly as if in a dream "What did you say?" she breathed.

"I said come home—"

"Before that," she said, her voice strained as she lowered her feet onto the floor. His warmth penetrated her as she brushed up against his leg. "The first part," she questioned him.

"I said it can work between us."

She placed a hand on his arm. "Say it again," she pleaded, her voice soft and unsure, almost nervous that she had misunderstood.

There was emotion in his expression as he leaned forward and drew her closer.

"I love you." He gathered her up into the strong warmth of his arms and took a seat on the couch with her lying across his lap. The steady drum of his heart reached straight to her own and mixed until they beat as one.

"I love you, too, London," she breathed, drinking in the scent that was so distinctly his.

He kissed the top of her head and whispered again that he loved her. "I want only you Bianca…all of you. To share my bed…to share my life." He pulled her into the circle of his arms and stroked her arm gently. "Bianca, let me give you my heart."

"Yes, London."

He placed her back onto the couch and nuzzled her neck as he whispered once again the words of love she had so longed to hear. She thought of all the days and nights they would spend together…him…her…their child.

Bianca recalled how many nights she had wondered what it would be like to really share a life together and for London to love her as she loved him. But her fantasy hadn't come anywhere close to this blissful reality.

"**SWEPT AWAY** proves that Ms. Forster is still at the top of the romance game."
—*Romantic Times BOOKreviews*

ESSENCE BESTSELLING AUTHOR

GWYNNE FORSTER

Swept Away

Veronica Overton was once one of the most respected women in Baltimore, but now her reputation is in ruins. With her confidence shattered, Veronica sets out to rebuild her life. Yet her search leads to family secrets— and ignites a smoldering attraction to Schyler Henderson. And not even their conflict and distrust of one another can cool the passion between them!

Coming the first week of May 2009
wherever books are sold.

ARABESQUE®

www.kimanipress.com
www.myspace.com/kimanipress   KPGFI590509

The neighborhood has never looked this good....

Kissing the *Man* next door

DEVON VAUGHN ARCHER

When sexy Ian Kelly moves next door to single mom
Mackenzie Brown, it's more than just the barbecue grill
that heats up. But when her teenage son returns from
living cross-country with her ex, Mackenzie wonders if
Ian is still enticed by her good-neighbor policy.

*Coming the first week of May 2009
wherever books are sold.*

KIMANI™
ROMANCE

www.kimanipress.com
www.myspace.com/kimanipress   KPDVA1150509

REQUEST YOUR FREE BOOKS!

2 FREE NOVELS
PLUS 2 FREE GIFTS!

KIMANI™
ROMANCE

Love's ultimate destination!

YES! Please send me 2 FREE Kimani™ Romance novels and my 2 FREE gifts (gifts are worth about $10). After receiving them, if I don't wish to receive any more books, I can return the shipping statement marked "cancel." If I don't cancel, I will receive 4 brand-new novels every month and be billed just $4.69 per book in the U.S. or $5.24 per book in Canada, plus 25¢ shipping and handling per book and applicable taxes, if any*. That's a savings of over 20% off the cover price! I understand that accepting the 2 free books and gifts places me under no obligation to buy anything. I can always return a shipment and cancel at any time. Even if I never buy another book from Kimani Press, the two free books and gifts are mine to keep forever.

168 XDN EF2D   368 XDN EF3T

Name _____ (PLEASE PRINT)

Address _____ Apt. #_____

City _____ State/Prov. _____ Zip/Postal Code_____

Signature (if under 18, a parent or guardian must sign)

Mail to **The Reader Service:**
IN U.S.A.: P.O. Box 1867, Buffalo, NY 14240-1867
IN CANADA: P.O. Box 609, Fort Erie, Ontario L2A 5X3

Not valid to current subscribers of Kimani Romance books.

**Want to try two free books from another line?
Call 1-800-873-8635 or visit www.morefreebooks.com.**

* Terms and prices subject to change without notice. N.Y. residents add applicable sales tax. Canadian residents will be charged applicable provincial taxes and GST. Offer not valid in Quebec. This offer is limited to one order per household. All orders subject to approval. Credit or debit balances in a customer's account(s) may be offset by any other outstanding balance owed by or to the customer. Please allow 4 to 6 weeks for delivery. Offer available while quantities last.

Your Privacy: Kimani Press is committed to protecting your privacy. Our Privacy Policy is available online at www.eHarlequin.com or upon request from the Reader Service. From time to time we make our lists of customers available to reputable third parties who may have a product or service of interest to you. If you would prefer we not share your name and address, please check here. ☐

KROM08R

The thirteenth novel in
the successful *Hideaway* series...

NATIONAL BESTSELLING AUTHOR

ROCHELLE ALERS

Secret Agenda

When Vivienne Neal's "perfect life" is turned
upside down, she moves to Florida to take a job
with Diego Cole-Thomas, a powerful CEO with
an intimidating reputation. Vivienne's job skills
prove invaluable to Diego, and on a business trip,
their relationship takes a sensual turn. But when
threatening letters arrive at Diego's office, he
realizes a horrible secret can threaten both of
them—and their future together.

"There's no doubt that Rochelle Alers is a compelling
storyteller who has the ability to weave romance with
the delicate subtlety of Monet."
—*Romantic Times BOOKreviews* on *HIDEAWAY*

*Coming the first week of May 2009
wherever books are sold.*

ARABESQUE®